Erin

by

Jerry B. Jenkins

MOODY PRESS

CHICAGO

Library of Congress Cataloging in Publication Data

Jenkins, Jerry B.
Erin.

(Margo mystery; #6)
I. Title.   II. Series: Jenkins, Jerry B.
(Margo mystery; #6)
[PS3560.E485M3 no. 6]   813′.54s [813′.54]   81-22368
ISBN 0-8024-4316-8   AACR2

To Larry Hanlon,
a kindred spirit

Chapter One

When your boss calls at four o'clock in the morning, you respond the way you would if he called at four in the afternoon. At least you should.

"Hello?" I said groggily.

"This is me," came the familiar voice of Earl Haymeyer, calling from just a few doors down the hall. We lived on the second floor of his two-story building, the floor that also housed his EH Detective Agency.

Earl sounded serious—appropriate, I thought, for waking someone.

"I need you to go with me to Proviso West High School in Hillside," he said.

"Right now?"

"Of course right now. You think I'm calling now to set a date for later? Johnny Bizell was found murdered in his car."

Johnny Bizell. I'd heard that name enough during the past several months. How many times had Earl's secretary, Bonnie, said Bizell was the one man she could kill without losing sleep over it?

"Shipman will meet us there, Philip," Earl was saying, "but we've gotta move. We'll be lucky if they haven't moved the body already."

"Margo going?" I asked, switching a light on and squinting.

"No. I'm enough of a chauvinist yet to think a woman might be better off not seeing this. Now Philip, let's go! I'll be waiting in the car."

I splashed water on my face and dragged a comb through my hair as I heard Earl's door shut and him trotting down the stairs. I didn't think it was fair for him to dress before calling me and then make me look slow. Two minutes later, wearing only blue jeans, a T-shirt, moccasins (no socks), and my trench coat, I slid into Earl's car.

"Bring your gun?" he asked.

"No. Should I?"

"No time. Forget it."

The night watchman who guarded the drug store, boutique, and professional offices in Earl's building tipped his cap as Earl swung out onto Glencoe Road to the Tri-State Tollway south.

"I got the call from an old nemesis of mine," Earl explained. "Chicago Homicide Detective Sergeant Walvoord F. Festschrift."

"What in the world kind of a name is that?"

"Who knows? Wally says his mother was Jewish, married a German, and always wanted to live in Holland."

"Do I wanna know what the *F* stands for?"

"Feinberg."

"Mercy. So what's the deal on Bizell, and why is Chicago in on it if it happened at a suburban high school?"

8

"I'm not sure yet. Festschrift was really gloating over the fact that he and I would be locking heads over this one. He was my first boss when I went plainclothes in Chicago. He's got a lot of ability but no ambition. He never wanted to be anything more than a homicide detective, and he's turned down promotion after promotion. Problem is, when the guys he's trained and brought along are then promoted over him because he won't take the promotions, he resents them."

"And that's what happened to you?"

"Yup. It was awkward to become his boss, but I always felt I treated him fairly. He was tough to supervise, though. Sarcastic. Condescending. Always accused me of being a glory-seeker."

"Were you?"

"Probably, but I hid it well."

"From everyone but Fet—"

"Festschrift."

"Right."

Earl drove on in silence, neither of us willing to mention the possibility that anyone we knew could have had anything to do with the murder of Johnny Bizell. When Earl exited to the Eisenhower east and we were just a few minutes from Hillside, I asked, "How did this Festschrift guy know to call you at all?"

"That's what I'd like to know."

We passed the Hillside Shopping Center and the front of the huge Proviso West Campus, a prime example of a sprawling educational plant that gives suburban kids advantages that few others enjoy. The events sign at the edge of the front lawn was still lit, and I shot a double take as I realized the implications: INTERNATIONAL GYM-NASTICS EXHIBITION TONITE ONLY.

"Erin?" I asked.

Earl pursed his lips and nodded.

"Bizell was here for that?"

"Apparently so."

"But still, how would Festschrift know of our connection, and why would Chicago Homicide—?"

"I don't know, Philip. I told you, I don't know."

Even at this early hour, a small group of onlookers had gathered, attracted by the police car and ambulance lights. "You can bet Wally doesn't have his dashlight on," Earl said. "Hates that kind of thing."

Earl was right. As we walked to the edge of a roped-off area near the field house, I spotted the unmarked Chicago police car. The blue light on the dash was dark. The suburban cars all had flashers going and an ambulance was backing into place, also lit up like a Christmas tree. The man I guessed to be Sgt. Festschrift was swearing.

"Get these lights off," he railed. "You wanna draw the whole town? Mi's well blow yer sirens too!"

Earl and I stood at the edge of the rope and watched the fat man. He wore giant rubber-soled black shoes and white socks, which you could see when they peeked from under his too-long and low-riding suit pants—pants that were baggy at the knees but too tight-waisted to cover his ample belly. One shirttail hung out, his tie was loose, and his hands were on his hips, pushing his overcoat and suit coat back. Beyond him about fifteen feet was the silver

10

Corvette of Johnny Bizell, the driver's side door open. I knew Bizell had to still be inside or close by, but I couldn't see from where we stood.

Finally, Festschrift noticed Earl and waddled over. "Let this man in," he told the uniformed officer at the rope.

"He's with me," Earl said, pointing at me. "Philip Spence."

"Yeah, yeah, good to know ya, Spence," Festschrift said, offering a meaty paw. He led us around the ambulance to the door of the 'Vette where the body of Johnny Bizell sat behind the wheel. The inside light was getting dimmer, indicating that he had sat there for hours. "It ain't pretty, Earl, but then these never are."

Earl was suddenly more polite than I'd ever seen him, asking Festschrift's permission before doing anything. Later he would tell me that this was merely the etiquette of the jungle and that if he had been in charge of the investigation, he would have expected the same treatment from Festschrift.

"Can I take a peek inside, Wally?"

"Yeah, but don't touch anything, and leave that murder weapon, such as it is, right where it lies."

I knew Earl would be offended that he was being told by a detective sergeant to not touch anything at a murder scene. As if Earl hadn't investigated dozens of murders in his career as a policeman, special investigator for the US attorney, and now a private detective. But he didn't let it show and motioned that I should follow him to the other side of the car.

We peered into the passenger side window, but the light from one of the parking lot lights reflected off it and distorted the view. We could see that Bizell's head lay back on the headrest and that his eyes were open. His right leg was over the hump on the floor and his right hand, covered with blood, rested outstretched in the seat.

From the edge of the roped-off area, Larry Shipman called to Earl. "Wally," Earl said, "that's another of my men. Can he join us?"

The sergeant appeared annoyed but let Shipman in. Larry, who's been around such things a lot more than I have, started taking notes and looking at every angle. After he was introduced to Festschrift, he plunged right in. "Hey, Sarge," he said, "how 'bout opening that passenger door? You can do it with a wire or something without affecting fingerprints."

"I know, kid," Festschrift said. "I ain't 'xactly a rookie myself, ya know. I got a team of forensic types comin' out here at dawn, and I don't want you rummies messin' up the crime scene for 'em."

"Then why did you call us?" Earl asked.

Festschrift looked as if he wanted to tell him right then and there but decided against it.

"Just let us have one closer look before you move the body," Earl said, dripping with deference, which his old companion ate up.

"Awright, but don't touch a thing."

Festschrift fished a hooked wire from his pocket and moved quickly to the passenger door. He fastened it to the handle without touching anything with his hands, and

12

gave a sharp yank. The door popped open and Earl leaned in, reaching out behind him without looking, as if he expected Festschrift to hand him something. Festschrift produced a flashlight.

"Philip," Earl called. I could hardly hear him with his head deep into the car and his back to me. I leaned in. Shipman was staring in from the other side of the car.

Violently deceased bodies are something I don't think I'll ever get used to. I once asked Earl how he got used to them. "I didn't," he said simply. But now he was bent over the passenger seat, his head a few inches from the wide-eyed face of a dead man whose blood had flooded the front left bucket seat, the console, and much of the rear floor. Earl backed out, nearly bumping me. He handed me the light. "Look on the floor between the seats," he said.

"Do I want to?"

He stared at me. I leaned in. Despite the great amount of blood, it was mostly dry, another clue to timing. The smell nauseated me. On the floor, right on the edge of a tiny pool of blood, was what appeared to be a small plastic toy, purple colored. I pointed the light directly at it and noticed a reflection, as if it had metal imbedded in it.

The death wound was a gash at the right side of Bizell's neck, and the blood had poured from him on that side. But his left hand, dangling at his side, also had a small laceration. Earl had noticed it too. As the paramedics moved into position to move the body and Festschrift supervised the shooting of several photographs, Earl and I hurried around to the other side of the car where we joined

13

Larry. "See that?" he whispered, pointing to the small tear in the victim's left hand. We nodded. "I have a theory," he said.

Festschrift approached. "Save it," Earl told Larry, handing the flashlight to the sergeant.

"You boys got time for some coffee?" the old cop asked.

"I s'pose," Earl said, "though I hate to be seen in public looking like this. But it's probably the only chance I'll get to find out what you're doing here, and why you called me."

"You got it," Festschrift said with a grin.

I felt greasy and grundy as we slid into a booth at a combination bakery and coffee shop at the nearby shopping center. We were the first customers of the morning. It didn't help much that I was jammed into a booth next to Sergeant Festschrift and sitting across from Haymeyer and Shipman, who were not successful in hiding their glee at my plight.

"So, this is your crew, huh, Earl?" Festschrift said, stuffing half a sweet roll into one side of his mouth and dousing it with coffee so hot that none of the rest of us had even dared get close enough to blow on it yet.

"Basically, Wally," Earl said. "I've also got a young woman, Margo Franklin, and we have a secretary/receptionist."

"I know," Wally said. "Mrs. Bonnie Murray, widowed several years, a couple of married daughters, one living in

14

Chicago named Linda Gibbons. Separated from her husband Greg. Has an only child, Erin, who is fast becoming the talk of international gymnastics."

"Uh-huh," Earl said slowly, an unbitten Danish melting in his fingers. "What else do you know, and more importantly, why?"

"I know that Johnny Bizell is the reason the Gibbonses are separated, and I know that the daughter Erin and the grandmother Bonnie have been none too thrilled that he has injured the marriage."

"So, what are you saying?"

"I'm saying I don't know what that little hunk of plastic and metal in the back seat of that 'Vette is yet, but something tells me that when I do, it's gonna lead to someone who had a reason to kill Johnny Bizell."

Shipman and I caught each other's eyes. Earl didn't flinch, but the topping on that Danish was dripping onto the table. "All right, Wally, for whatever problems you and I may have had in the past, we've always been straight with each other, and we're both after the same thing, so why don't you tell me exactly what you're up to."

"You gonna eat that Danish, Earl?" Wally said, stalling. Earl handed it to him and watched it disappear in another wash of coffee. Festschrift leaned forward and across me to grab an ashtray, pushing the table into Earl and Larry's ribs. He lit a cigarette, took a deep drag, squinted as he pushed his chin in the air, and blew a blue cloud over our heads. He placed the cigarette carefully on the edge of the tray and wriggled out of his overcoat, exposing a dark green suit, frayed at the cuffs and worn at the elbows, that looked as if it had been on the job as long as he had.

"You're wonderin' why Chicago is in on a suburban murder, is that it?"

Earl nodded, apparently annoyed at Festschrift's dramatics. The fat man wanted Earl to have to drag it out of him, but Earl wouldn't bite.

"OK, Earl," Wally said, finally. "We know as much about the Gibbons situation as you do. You know because you want to keep your secretary informed. We know because Bizell is a Chicagoan with mob ties."

"We guessed that," Earl said. "But why the inordinate interest?"

"The Vice Control Division has had Bizell under surveillance for some time and they just kept a portfolio on his contacts. When they noticed that you and your people were tailing him too, they wanted to know why. It wasn't hard to find out. When Bizell turns up dead, I inherit the case. And my first suspects may be friends of yours, maybe even co-workers." Festschrift looked at each of us with a slight smile. Haymeyer continued to stare.

"You want me as an ally in this investigation, or an adversary?" Earl asked, eager to switch to the offensive.

"Do I have a choice? Do *you* have a choice? You might want to be my ally, Earl, but when I start poking around your office, suspecting your secretary and your secretary's son-in-law, and asking everyone in your shop what Bonnie Murray has said about the now dead home wrecker, we'll be adversaries whether you want to be or not."

"Are you seriously suspecting my secretary?"

"You see, Earl? Your secretary is the best suspect I've had on a homicide in three years, and you can't see it because she's an employee and, I imagine, a friend. But think about it. The woman surely has a motive. She's not a small person, so with the right means she could conceivably have done the job. The lab will tell us if that 'weapon' in the backseat was the means. You want me to tell you about her opportunity? Can't have a murder unless you've got a motive, means, and opportunity."

"Let me guess," Larry interrupted. "You're gonna tell us that Bonnie was at Proviso West last night for the gymnastics meet. Well, so were thousands of others, and few with as good a reason as the grandmother of the women's all-around champion."

"Anyway," I said, wishing later I hadn't, "Margo was there with her." Larry and Earl looked at me as if I had lost my mind, volunteering information like that. Chicago Homicide Detective Sergeant Walvoord F. Festschrift merely smiled.

"And when can I meet this Margo?" he asked.

Chapter Two

It was due only to my own foolishness that Margo and I were not still engaged. Sure, she had been childish, insecure, fickle, but then what did I expect? I knew her background. She had never had a normal adolescence, if there is such a thing.

She had seen her parents' marriage break up, had for years carried the dark secret that her mother was a murderer, finally exposed her, and then saw her die in prison. In many ways, Margo Franklin was an emotional cripple, yet I spent so much time trying to convince her that I didn't feel sorry for her or pity her and that my love for her was genuine and simply inspired by the person she was, that I actually began to believe it.

It was largely true, but Margo was *due* some pity. I should have seen that. I should have been able to let her be what she was, a deep girl, rich in character and inner beauty (not to mention outer), but who needed time, even at this stage of her life, to grow up, to find herself in the truest sense.

But I had not been patient. She had wanted time to think. The small, dark, fine-boned and delicately featured beauty had virtually disappeared from my life. I saw her every day in the office, and we were more than cordial.

The difficult, uncomfortable time was past. We were now fairly good friends, but I'd rather it had remained uncomfortable. Because I knew now, more than ever, that I loved her deeply.

It hurt me to see her grow emotionally and especially spiritually and to know, first, that I had nothing to do with it, and second, that I wasn't even seeing it firsthand. And yeah, OK, I wondered if she had a new mentor, someone who had swept her off her feet, some super-spiritual type who could be all and more to her than she needed.

But she didn't. She never dated, as far as I could tell. She was very active in a small church, and although I considered switching from the large church we used to attend together, I knew she would feel threatened. I wanted her to feel loved, not threatened.

Around the office, everyone could sense a selflessness in her that was attractive, not obnoxious. She was not putting on just for attention; she really did think of others first. Even in talking to me, she would ask and ask and ask and rarely tell. You could talk to her for twenty minutes and go away feeling good about yourself, only to realize later that you had learned nothing about her, except that she was something special.

So now I was ready with my pity, and she was no longer in need of it. I was more understanding of what she had been going through, and she was no longer going through it. She had even become accurately introspective. I'll never forget the night she called and asked if I could meet her somewhere to chat. I thought she was ready for us to get back together.

But she didn't even know that that's what I wanted. Maybe if she knew, she could start thinking about it too— But that wasn't even on her mind. In fact, when I suggested a few meeting places that she had to associate with our betrothal days, she politely declined and we settled on neutral ground. We met in the lobby of her apartment building.

For the first several minutes she asked me about myself. Of course she knew the day-to-day stuff, but she asked about my parents, my new car, my feelings about Earl's having talked me into carrying a gun (he had talked her into the same thing, but dumb me didn't think to ask how *she* felt about it), and about my plans for the future.

My plans, I told her, included simply doing the best job I could for Earl, learning as much as I could from him, and just growing where I was planted. She asked about church and even my spiritual life. I was taken aback, yet there was no gall, no guile. It made me uncomfortable, probably because I knew she was surging ahead of me by leaps and bounds.

I told her I was still hangin' in there, and I could tell by the look on her face that she knew I was being purposefully vague. Then she finally began to talk about herself. She went on for about five minutes about how God had apparently used our "crisis" to put her where He wanted her. Well, He hadn't put her where *I* wanted her, but on the other hand, I knew that was selfish and that I certainly couldn't argue with how she had grown as a whole person.

"My point in telling you all this," she had concluded,

"is just to let you know that I wanted time, and I got it, and I'm glad. God has used it. I've learned that Christianity is not a part of life that can be compartmentalized. It's not a filter through which we view everything else. It is life. It's everything *and* everything else."

I was tempted to unkindly ask who she had been reading lately, but something told me that this was the mind I had always appreciated in her—loved, in fact. This was the analytical bearing of a person who had endured dark times in her life and had been forced to evaluate them and make sense of them.

"So, I want you to know how special you are and will always be to me, Philip. I will never forget you and your struggling faith, and your caring and your love. And of course I can never thank you enough for introducing me to God. I know what a pill I was, and for sure, I can't say that's entirely behind me now, but you deserve more than an apology. I have no more to give, so you have at least that, and I want you to forgive me."

I was speechless. Forgive her? Somehow in light of that request I couldn't remember what a rascal she had indeed been at times. Her impulsiveness, her lack of logic, her verbal cruelty all came into perspective somehow. I'm not saying she was right or had excuses, but she did have reasons. And I had harbored bitterness in spite of them.

I had wanted to take her in my arms that night, tell her I loved her and that she never had to ask my forgiveness for anything, but I was frozen. She had not called me to make up with me, to become attached to me again, to melt me back into a relationship. She was serious, she was sincere.

She had seen herself for what she was and had simply asked forgiveness.

She repeated her request and all I could do was nod. She thanked me for coming, carried the rest of the conversational pleasantries so I could leave without making a fool of myself, and that was that.

For the next several days I had tried to get next to her, to be her special friend, at least, in the office. But she treated everyone the same. I tried catching her eye and smiling at her, and without being unkind she simply smiled right back, just as she did for everyone else. I couldn't hold her gaze the way I had been able to when we were in love. That hurt, but she hadn't intended it to. If she had intended to freeze me out, she easily could have, and it would have made it simpler for me.

Earl was concerned that we not let our love problems surface at the office. We were aware that few establishments even allow engaged couples to work together. But she was so oblivious to my feelings for her that any formality or coolness in front of others was eliminated. She treated me the way she treated everyone else, and *everyone* loved her.

I would ask her out, she would ask if it would be all right if three or four of us went together, and I didn't want to be a sourpuss by saying no. I had made my feelings clear to her when we broke up, and she had believed me. I didn't know how to express to her that I had been wrong and was sorry. Perhaps if I hadn't seen such a change in her, I wouldn't have changed my mind. Did that mean my love for her was conditional? I didn't know. Conditi or not, it was there now and stronger than ever, and I needed a way to prove it to her.

She had begun spending a lot of time with Bonnie. Bonnie lived alone on another floor in Margo's building. She had asked Earl and Larry to check on her daughter Linda's husband, because Linda had told Bonnie that Greg was being unfaithful. She had been terribly hurt by the knowledge that it was Linda who had been seeing another man.

The investigation proved that rather than Greg Gibbons's seeing one of the secretaries from his office, Linda was seeing Johnny Bizell, the leading salesman in Greg's office. Needless to say, Bonnie was horrified, and Margo spent much of her time trying to convince Bonnie that she could not blame herself.

Mostly, Bonnie was worried about Greg and Linda's daughter, Erin, who had recently turned fourteen. Not long after Earl and Larry had told Bonnie what they found, Linda and this Johnny Bizell—one of those great-looking forty-year-old bronze types from the covers of fashion catalogs—quit being so careful to cover their tracks.

Erin had seen him at the apartment a couple of times and recognized him from her father's office. When she raised the question in front of both parents, things deteriorated rapidly. Linda finally admitted the relationship but insisted that it was over. For about a month, it appeared she was telling the truth. Greg had moved out, and divorce proceedings had begun, but things stalled when it appeared that Linda was no longer seeing Bizell.

How Greg was able to work in the same office with Johnny, I'll never know, but I guess except for their common "appreciation" of the same woman and their selling of the same office equipment products, they ran in entirely different circles. At least, that's what I gathered from what Sgt. Festschrift had said early Saturday morning.

What had really complicated matters was that the press had become aware of the marriage problems. None of the details (like Bizell's name or even that Linda was seeing someone else) were printed, but the fact of the separation was public. Why? Because of Erin.

She had been interested in gymnastics since she was a tiny child after having seen first Olga Korbut and then Nadia Comaneci in the Olympics on television. In spite of the fact that Greg was never into big money and Linda even had to work part time to help make ends meet, they scraped up enough to send Erin to gymnastics camp a couple of years in a row, let her join the school team, and finally signed her up on a local AAU team.

That team had a traveling squad of the best eight girls who competed throughout the midwest, but it also carried three or four dozen other girls and gave them a place to learn and work out and train. When Erin was eight, nine, and ten years old and had been in the program for several years, she talked her parents into taking her to the meets so she could watch the traveling squad and cheer for them. Greg was never much interested in it because he couldn't envision his gangly little daughter ever reaching that level, but Linda had taken her to the nearby meets.

Something happened in Erin's mind when she saw her older friends begin to really, truly improve and become competitive under the tutelage of their coach, Nik Adamski. At first her friends were embarrassing, but through the years as they grew in strength and grace, and as their parents allowed them more time for workouts, their scores started edging upward. The dozens of girls under the traveling squad who made up the rest of the team began to see themselves as teammates, and they exulted as much as the participants with each victory.

As an older girl moved up or out or off to college, someone from the lower levels would be chosen to replace her. Not even Erin remembers when she started to foresee that possibility for herself. She had always performed in the lower half of the fifty or so girls in the practice meets that were held for parents' eyes only. But then she asked permission to train the year around.

Most of the parents of the other girls were well-to-do and fully supported their daughters, sending them for expensive specialized training over the summer. Greg and Linda could not afford that, but they were able to sponsor Erin's staying on the team all year every year. And she began to improve.

By the time she was twelve, she had moved into the top fifteen, and then, her grandmother says because her father finally took an interest, she blossomed. She grew a couple of inches, gained a little strength and a lot of self-confidence. And finally—her coach attributes this to his brainwashing—she developed a singlemindedness for excellence in her sport that transcended everything else in her life.

She ate, drank, and slept gymnastics. There were only four Olympic events, she reminded her mother often, and she would perfect them all. She became a marvelous free exerciser and vaulter, and Coach Adamski began to push harder for her to reach her potential on the uneven bars and the beam.

He worked with her all one summer, and when competition began in the fall, she was the first alternate. She worked out all week just like the rest of the first team, but week after week she failed to compete in any meets. No one was injured or sick and she was unable to sneak in past the last girl on the squad during pre-meet tryouts. What was worse (or better, depending on your perspective), the entire team was getting better.

Nik Adamski had worked his magic over the years and had built one of the most respected gymnastics programs in the country. For two years running they were national AAU champions and sent four young women on to the national team to compete overseas and host meets in the US. The girls below Erin were getting better, and the girls on the first team were internationally ranked. She came to the slow realization that at the tender age of twelve she was ninth woman on the best team in the United States and among the best fifty or sixty women gymnasts in the world, yet she had never competed in an actual meet.

One of the girls Erin idolized was the best gymnast Nik Adamski had ever coached. Larisa Cumiskey, sixteen the summer Erin turned twelve, had strength and grace and precision that won her the all-around competition in every national meet she entered. Internationally, she was always a threat, winning at least one event and finishing high in the overall standings each time.

The other girls would sit wide-eyed listening to Larisa tell about competing in Poland and the USSR and Czechoslovakia and Germany. Everyone wanted to be Larisa's friend, and most were, at least those on the first team. Somehow she had been able to avoid the haughtiness that so often accompanies brilliance. Erin decided that if she could ever get next to Larisa, she could help make her a great gymnast too. But Larisa had been on the same team for years and had seemed to hardly notice little Erin.

Then came the week that Erin showed such class and flair in vaulting that, in front of everybody, Nik Adamski told the last vaulter on the first team that if he were selecting only the best competitors in each event and not the best all-around performances, she would have lost her place on the team.

That girl didn't burst into tears and run from the room. Instead she agreed and shook her head in admiration of the tiny twelve-year-old who had drawn applause from the whole team. Larisa and the others gathered around Erin and patted her on the head and the back, encouraging her to keep working hard.

When the excitement died down, Nik said in his broken English, "I vant volunteer or two to vork vit' dis girl. She been close to first team for too long and is now ready for big move."

Erin could have died when Larisa Cumiskey stepped forward and said, "I'll work with Erin." It was the start of an unusual friendship.

Chapter Three

According to Margo, who had grown close to Bonnie and thus to Erin and even her friend Larisa, the older girl really took Erin under her wing.

After practice every afternoon—and sometimes, with permission, even during practice—Larisa would personally coach Erin on the uneven bars. Where Coack Nik was a shouter, a demanding, team-oriented, Dutch uncle type, Larisa had her own brand of praise and encouragement.

Nik enforced unity on the team, insisting that there be no jealousy, no territorial protection even in this highly individualized sport. It was probably the reason Larisa had volunteered to help the young upstart. She had learned her lesson well and truly believed that it was the togetherness Nik had fostered that had made their team the best in the country. And if this little girl could improve that last 10 percent that could make her superb, the team would be that much better.

During the Christmas vacation, there was no meet competition and Nik held only a few practice sessions. But Larisa and Erin were at the gym for several hours each day, getting to know each other, but more importantly, pushing Erin to heights she had never imagined possible. The age difference was just right, because she held such a reverence for her mentor that any praise she could elicit was that much more meaningful.

When Erin flew through a stratospheric routine on the uneven bars, Larisa was exultant. "Erin, that was a nine-point-oh if I ever saw one. I am not kidding, Erin, you've arrived."

Erin was redfaced, hardly believing it. The years she had invested in dreaming and working hard at the fundamentals Nik drilled into the team everyday had given her a base upon which to add creativity and courage. "Now all you need is abandon on both the beam and the bars," Larisa said.

"Abandon?"

"Right. Let yourself go. Lose your tentativeness, your last shred of fear. You're good, now believe it. You've been trained well by a great coach, and you're not going to hurt yourself. Start adding daring and speed to every move until you're confident and can nail a dangerous routine as easily as you do a normal one."

Erin was eager to try it, and within ten days she was flying through routines that thrilled her. When the coach and the rest of the team returned for an all-team tryout before the next meet, Erin seemed to have grown up overnight. The advice that had moved her from being good to excellent on the bars and the beam had made her among the best three on the team in floor ex and vault.

All of a sudden, Erin was a first-team member of the defending national championship women's gymnastics team, and she could hardly wait for her first meet. Yet when it came it was an exhibition against some of the best gymnasts in the world. She wasn't expected to place in any of her events. Indeed, it would be a chore for even Larisa to win anything but the uneven bars.

When it was over, the best performance by a US team member was a 9.7 on the bars, good for third place, by Larisa. Erin choked and was unable to produce the same daring she had exhibited during workouts. In her best event, the floor ex, her 8.6 didn't even put her in the top ten. She missed her dismount off the beam and landed on her seat. She stubbed her toes at the start and in the middle of her uneven bars routine. Her vaulting was uninspired. She was humiliated.

In the locker room after the meet, Larisa and a couple of other girls tried to console her. "You don't wanna know what my first meet scores were, Erin," one said. "I didn't even crack an eight until my third meet, I was so scared."

"I didn't feel scared," Erin insisted through her tears. "I just couldn't do what I wanted to do!"

"That's what scared feels like," another said. "There are a lot of girls who would love to have had your all-around score tonight."

Within four more meets, Erin Gibbons was the second best gymnast on her team in every event. By the end of the year, she was within five hundredths of a point of Larisa in the vault and floor ex and within two tenths on the bars and beam. And they were closer than ever as friends.

When Larisa returned from off-season international competition, she found a thirteen-year-old who had not only drawn to within an eyelash of her in every event, but who also had begun to shave her legs and wear makeup, emulating her idol, her teammate, and her rival in every respect. "My mom won't let me wear the makeup except during meets," she said, and Larisa and her friends laughed. "She thinks I need to look older to the judges or they won't believe they're seeing a good routine."

Erin confided to Margo once that she and Larisa had had a good heart-to-heart talk during the wee hours at a slumber party in the mansion home of Ernest and Jean Cumiskey. Larisa told Erin that she should never let their friendship come in the way of their competition, that they could continue to like and respect each other while striving their hardest to beat each other. "Our team will only benefit from it," Larisa said. "I was raised to be number one, and that means someday I'd like to be the best in the world, but if you wind up better than I am, then we'll be one and two. I don't mind telling you I'd rather be first, but we may be the only real competition each other has this year. We can keep our team winning by trying to outdo each other."

The girls also shared family secrets. Erin was already suspecting the future of her parents' marriage because of continued fights and threats. Then she was convinced her mother was seeing a man from her father's office. She even learned his name—Johnny Bizell—and knew his car, a late model silver Corvette.

Larisa's problems seemed to pale in comparison. While the greatest embarrassment to Erin, outside her mother's deceit, was that she could hardly bring a bunch of friends to a small apartment for a party, slumber or otherwise, Larisa's was that she had a stage father.

Her mother wasn't too bad at the meets. She was proud of her daughter and often had to restrain herself from charging onto the floor and hugging her when she won an event or a meet, but it was Larisa's father, Ernest, who was the talk of the circuit.

"He wants me to be number one worse than I do," Larisa once told Erin. "He believes in being number one so deeply that it drives him crazy that my little brothers are twins. I think he actually favors Bobby over Billy because he appeared eight minutes sooner nine years ago. When he watches them play junior hockey or soccer or baseball or football, he's thrilled if one of them is the best, but he's obsessed with the fact that the other is not."

Sometimes Larisa laughed about it; other times she did not. Finally the day came when Erin had to ask, "Has your father's attitude toward me changed since I started to give you more competition?"

"I don't think he ever had an attitude about you," Larisa said. "I know his attitude toward me has sure changed since you've been coming on. He's forever badgering me about my diet, my sleeping habits, everything. He wants to know if I'm working out as much as I used to. He wants to know if my age has affected my weight or muscle tone. I'm only seventeen years old and he fears I'll be over the hill by the time the next Olympics rolls around. He doesn't realize that once you get into the high nines, it's hard to improve without getting tens. He says my goal should be to break Nadia's record of seven perfect scores in one Olympic game. I've yet to score one ten in competition. It's not good enough for me to be the best in the US or even in the world. I have to be the best in history, and now it looks like you'll keep me from that."

Larisa put her arm around Erin's shoulder to show that she didn't really mind the competition. "Anyway, why did you ask? Has Daddy acted differently around you lately?"

"Oh, yeah, if it's not just my imagination. He used to greet me, talk to me a little—mostly about you, of course—but now he acts like I'm not here."

Margo talked the rest of the staff into going to a six-team invitational meet in Chicago one night, and it happened to be the night that Erin edged Larisa in an event for the first time. Larisa still won the all-around, but Erin was a close second after topping her by a tenth of a point in, of all things, the uneven bars—Larisa's best event.

I don't know gymnastics except what I remember from high school and a little of the Olympics on television, but from what I could see, Larisa made no mistakes on her routine. She scored in the high nines, but Erin really flew. It was worth the extra tenth of a point, I guess. In fact, I thought Erin did better on the floor exercise than Larisa too, but the judges didn't agree.

It wasn't long after that that Erin and Larisa visited Erin's grandmother Bonnie at our office. They were going to go shopping late in the afternoon on a non-practice day. I was intrigued by the lithe little things, so close and yet such competitors. Their figures were so youthful, yet their calves were taut and their hands calloused and bony. They were just about to leave when Larisa's mother called to tell her that her father was insisting that she work out that night at the gym, even if it had to be alone.

She was in tears when she left, assuring Erin that it was all right and that she didn't mind not going shopping. Erin offered to work out with her, but Larisa wouldn't hear of it. "Maybe this way, Daddy will think I'm getting the jump on you," she said, trying to smile.

"You probably will be," Erin said. "Maybe I'd *better* come along." But she didn't.

What impressed me through it all was that both girls seemed to excel in spite of their parental problems.

I kind of got hooked on gymnastics, especially when Bonnie's granddaughter was competing, and Larry Shipman and I took in several meets whenever we could. We were there when Erin first tied Larisa for an overall first place. Larisa had won the uneven bars competition by two tenths and Erin had won the floor ex by the same margin. They had tied on the other two events, and you should have seen them beaming on the victory stand, arm in arm, waving.

Larisa's father was furious and drove home by himself, leaving his wife and two sons to fend for themselves. Was Jean Cumiskey embarrassed! She got a ride with Bonnie. I never heard what she said to her husband later, but I can imagine.

A real battle was shaping up for the national AAU finals, which were to be held at the University of Illinois Chicago Circle Campus. Wide World of Sports was there to tape the competition, and the place was a madhouse. I was really becoming an aficionado. Getting to know Erin better was a joy, and you can't get to know Erin without getting to know Larisa. They are inseparable, and I decided Larisa was one classy young lady—a truly beautiful person, a lot more like her mother than her father.

He was president of a national sales organization, and he looked the part. Everything he did and said (and wore) exuded class and the looking-out-for-number-one mentality. He found it impossible to talk to anyone about anything without categorizing, prioritizing, sizing up, and finding out where you fit in, whether you were number one or had the potential to be number one, and how you planned on getting there. He also found it impossible to talk for more than three minutes without bragging on Larisa, which I thought was OK, except that he seemed to take the credit for her excellence when I was convinced it was in spite of him.

Anyway, Larisa won the national all-around title, even though she finished third in one event and second in two others. A girl from Dubuque surprised everyone by winning the balance beam competition. Erin was second, a fraction ahead of Larisa. Erin finished first in floor ex and the vault, giving her more gold medals than anyone, but Larisa again was just a fraction behind in each event, and when she finally hit a perfect score on the uneven bars, it gave her enough margin to overcome Erin for the aggregate.

Strangely, however, the talk of the meet—mostly because of the national TV coverage—was of the thirteen-year-old teammate of the great Larisa Cumiskey who had come within a point and a half of winning four gold medals. A great deal of time was spent explaining not how Larisa had salvaged the all-around gold with a rare 10, but how close Erin had come to a dramatic sweep of the meet.

Larisa's experience in international competition aided her when she and Erin both made the United States team and competed around the world. In two meets, Larisa and Erin finished first and second to give the US women's team its first international victories ever. In other meets they finished second and third, usually with Larisa on top, but everyone knew, because of age, that Erin was fast becoming the top female gymnast in the United States, and that world recognition would not be far off.

Erin finally pushed her way past Larisa for the first time the Friday night before Johnny Bizell was found murdered. I had been with Earl and Larry at a White Sox game, and we hadn't returned to our apartments until nearly midnight.

Now, having been awakened by Earl at four and having met the reknowned Sgt. Festschrift, I wanted to read the paper and go back to bed. "We've got to find Bonnie," Earl said as he parked back at his building.

"I'll try to call her," I promised. "What else can we do? If she's not at home, she may be out with Margo or with Erin and Larisa."

"That's all we need," Earl said, yawning. "I want to get to all of them before Wally Festschrift does."

"If *we* can't find 'em, *he* sure can't," I said.

"Don't kid yourself," Earl said. "They could be being fingerprinted right now."

I laughed. He didn't.

"I'm going to be in the office this morning waiting for the lab report," he said, "so I'll try to reach the gals by phone. Get some sleep. We may be in for a lot of overtime the next few days. I told Larry he could go back to bed, so fair's fair."

"When you gonna get some sleep, Earl?"

"I never sleep. You know that."

I jogged down to the corner for a newspaper, then flopped onto my bed to read myself back to sleep. It wasn't easy. The front page carried the story of Johnny Bizell's death and Festschrift's intimation that it may have been a gangland hit. I knew as well as he did that he didn't believe that for a minute. Nothing about the murder looked clean enough for a mob job, but talking like that was his way of taking the heat off his real suspects, and off Earl too, though Earl was too smart for that. Festschrift thought Bonnie had the best motive—I couldn't argue with that—and he didn't want the media or anyone else in his way while he made his case. Everyone else, he hoped, would be looking the other way when he closed in on the real murderer.

The sports page mercifully buried the story of the White Sox late inning loss to the Yankees under a splash for Erin Gibbons, the new sensation, who "thrilled the hometown Chicago crowd at Proviso West High School last night with a quartet of 9.85s on the balance beam, the uneven parallel bars, floor exercise, and the vault to win all four events and the all-around gold, carrying the US women to victory" over four visiting European teams.

Larisa Cumiskey, now regarded as a "veteran," finished no lower than fourth in any event and won a silver in the all-around competition.

I wondered if Erin would get to enjoy her victory before hearing of the news of Johnny Bizell. Would it add to her euphoria? Or would she not be surprised in the least?

Chapter Four

I found it difficult to sleep, wondering why—even on the sports page—the newsmen felt it necessary to point out that Erin's performance was even more impressive, given the fact that she was from a broken home and had been raised in an apartment, no less. What would they do if they found out that the home wrecker had been murdered?

Earl called at about noon and asked me to join him and Larry at the office. He had heard nothing from Wally Festschrift about the lab report yet, but he wanted to prepare some charts to determine everyone's whereabouts the night before, starting with the time work ended.

"I haven't been able to reach Margo or Bonnie," Earl said. "For all I know, Wally has already gotten to Linda and Erin Gibbons."

"Did you try calling *them*?" Larry asked.

"Naw. I hardly know 'em. Anyway, I don't want to irritate Wally just now. He'd really be hot if I started questioning people before he did. I *would* like to see their reactions to the news, though. Anyway, let's get to work."

Earl used a felt-tipped marker and wrote several names on a big sheet of white cardboard.

He started with himself, Larry, and me. He wrote, "work, Peppercorn's for dinner, White Sox Park, home."

Then he wrote "Bonnie, work, home, Margo's for dinner, Proviso West, home."

"I know they went together. Do you guys know who drove?"

"Margo," I offered.

"You sure?"

I nodded. "That was the plan. And Erin was supposed to come back with them and stay with her grandmother."

"Are you serious?" Earl asked. "What about Larisa? They're usually inseparable."

"I don't know. I didn't hear anything about her coming back with them."

"Where would they be now?"

"Who knows?"

"Something bothers me about their relationship," Shipman said. "Doesn't it seem a little too good to be true? Larisa's eighteen goin' on nineteen, will graduate from high school this June; Erin just turned fourteen and won't start high school until this fall. Yet they seem to get along. The only thing they have in common is gymnastics."

I tried to explain it to him the way Margo had tried to explain it to me. Gymnastics can't be described as an "only thing." It's too much more than that. It's such a huge part of life to these girls, especially at this level, that everything else seems insignificant. "The biggest thing is that I think Erin has won Larisa's respect and even admiration, more than just for what she can do on the apparatus,

44

but by her courage and determination and all that. Plus, remember they have traveled the world together in competition."

"Yeah," Larry said, "but maybe I'm more realistic. Does it make sense that Larisa's not jealous or even contemptuous of a little girl who's stealing her thunder?"

"That's not as much realism as cynicism," I said.

Earl interrupted. "We're getting nowhere. We have to take Erin and Larisa's relationship at face value until we see or learn otherwise. While you're in the mood for talking, Ship, why don't you tell us your theory about the wound to Johnny Bizell's hand you were so hot about last night?"

"I wasn't so hot about it. It just made me visualize the murder, that's all."

"Now you're psychic," I teased.

Larry explained. "My guess is that the assailant inflicted the neck wound from the driver's side of the car, probably leaning in through the window."

"The door was open," Earl countered.

"And the wound was on the right side," I said.

Larry held up a hand to silence us. "But there was a wound in the victim's left hand. My guess is that the lab guys will find tissue on the inside door handle where Johnny tried desperately to get out."

"But why would he get out of the car on the side where his assailant is standing?"

"For one thing, the assailant wouldn't have still been standing there. The weapon, or most of it, is still in the car. The death wound was inflicted in one move, and there was nothing more the perpetrator could have done to have wounded Bizell any worse. He probably sensed that and ran off as Bizell reached up to his neck with his right hand—thus the bloodiness of it—and tried to jump out of the car, either for help or to get a better angle on stopping the bleeding.''

"I still don't see why he wouldn't have tried to avoid the assailant by heading out the other door," I said.

"Well, the car has bucket seats and a stick shift on the console. Even with all that adrenalin flowing, Bizell must have known he didn't have time to navigate *that* obstacle course.''

"Why couldn't the murderer have come in from the passenger's side and murdered him that way?" Earl asked, not challenging, just trying to draw a bead on Larry's logic.

"He could have, but it appears to me that the murder was a surprise. Bizell probably wasn't sure what was happening until it happened. And opening that door so frantically that he injured himself doing it proves that he probably did it after he was mortally wounded. If he had seen someone coming after him from the other side, he probably could have gotten out and escaped injury.''

"It's a long shot," Earl said. "But interesting, and you're thinking.''

"Thank you, teacher," Larry mocked. Earl ignored him.

"We don't really know what happened, then, to anyone else, including Bonnie and Margo, after we saw them leave work," Earl said.

Larry and I shook our heads, and Earl drew big question marks after their names. We heard heavy footsteps coming up the stairs and wheeled around to see Wally Festschrift burst through the door in the same tacky outfit he'd worn that morning. "My sentiments exactly," he said, huffing and puffing from the climb and motioning to Earl's chart with an unlit cigarette.

"Just tryin' to do our jobs," Earl said.

"Yeah, well, me too," Wally said. "May I?" he asked, dragging a chair between his legs and engulfing it with his body. Earl didn't respond. "So, where is everybody?"

"Everybody who?" Earl said.

"C'mon, Haymeyer," Festschrift said, "what're ya doing, harboring every suspect I got? I ain't found anybody but Greg Gibbons, and that poor sucker is disappointed that he *wasn't* responsible for Bizell's death."

"Are you sure he wasn't?"

"Positive. He's got an airtight alibi. He went to that tumbling meet or whatever you call it at the high school last night, but right afterward he had a meeting—guess where—with Larisa Cumiskey's old man." Wally put the still unlit cigarette between his lips and dug around in several pockets to produce a bent up notepad. "Ernest, Ernest Cumiskey is after Gibbons for a job with his company. Likes the young guy a lot, I guess."

"That doesn't compute," I blurted. Earl put his finger to his lip, but Festschrift caught it.

"Don't shush him, Lieutenant," Wally said, referring to Earl's rank when he was Festschrift's boss years before. "I thought we were all in this thing together and you got

47

nothin' to hide and all that. Why doesn't it compute, kid?"

I looked to Earl for permission. He was giving me one of those you-got-yourself-into-this-get-yourself-out-of-it looks. "I just can't imagine Ernest Cumiskey in the mood to talk business after his daughter had humiliated him in the gymnastics meet."

"I read in the paper that she finished second in the all-around," Shipman said.

"You don't understand," I said. "In her father's eyes, that's worse than breaking a leg. I've seen him so angry after meets where she's lost just one event that he will leave his family behind to find their own way home."

"Gibbons said Cumiskey seemed a little nervous," Wally said, "but that was all. He didn't represent it as anger, just preoccupation. I'll tell you frankly, I think Gibbons is just happy with the way his job interview went—and since you're not gonna bite and ask where they were, I'll tell ya. At our little breakfast spot."

"Charming," Earl said, intimating that he had heard nothing constructive so far. "You were going to call me with the lab findings."

"Well, hey, ain't an in-person performance better than a call? You should be flattered."

"I couldn't be more," Earl said dryly.

Festschrift flipped a few more pages in his grimy note-pad and tossed it onto Bonnie's desk where he could read from it while he finally lit up. Earl moved to open a window and let a cool breeze in. "I was gonna take my coat off," Festschrift whined. "Now I gotta leave it on."

"Suit yourself," Earl said.

"So, anyway, the autopsy shows that there was an initial wound at the front of the right side of the neck that left almost an inch-deep gash. In what they think was a simultaneous action, a slicing wound extended from that initial puncture back about an inch and a quarter, deep enough and long enough to sever both the carotid artery and the jugular vein."

"I've heard of going for the jugular," Shipman said. "What does the carotid artery do?"

"I'm glad you asked that, kid," Festschrift said, gesturing with both hands. "I've been wanting to show off my medical knowledge ever since I learned this. The veins carry blood back to the heart. The arteries take it away from the heart. Whoever pulled this job knew what he—or she—was doing. Those two workhorses, the jugular and the carotid, do the job on blood to and from the heart and brain. If only one or the other had been affected, Johnny's reflex action to stop the bleeding might have helped. But with the blood flow to and from the brain crippled, he lost the facility to do anything for himself."

"What did the coroner think about the wound to the left hand?" Shipman asked.

Festschrift slowed him down. "I'll get to that. Don't you want to know more about the death wound? The coroner says it was caused by a combination of something as sharp as a razor and as blunt as something fibrous. When we showed him the hunk from the backseat, it was like the last piece of a puzzle. Exhibit A. The lab guys would like to find a duplicate so they don't have to wash it or take it apart. They can't get a fingerprint off the plastic part, and although they have taken a couple of chips of the blood from it, they want to leave it as is. There is, they are sure, a razor blade imbedded in it."

"A homemade weapon?" Earl asked.

"They don't know for sure. We'll know soon, though. These guys are unbelievable."

"Yeah, they can trace almost anything," Larry said, "like the cause of a wound on a dead man's left hand?"

"Awright, awright, the coroner says that was caused by a blunt instrument, likely metal. Guys on the scene found tissue on the door handle and the coroner is satisfied that that's the solution."

Larry beamed and looked at Earl and me. It was a nice piece of deduction on his part, but I wasn't sure it told us anything substantial.

"Have they determined when Bizell died?" I asked.

"They're not entirely sure, but given the location of his car, it could have been during or after that gymnastics thing. He was really in a spot back there where none of the spectators getting in their cars could have seen him or the assailant. The coroner put the time of death at before midnight but he's only guessing how much before."

"How was he discovered?"

"A local squad car cruises through the parking lot every few hours, and the cop on that beat said he thought he saw a light glowing between the air-conditioning units and the garbage bins the first time around, but he didn't really check it out until his second time through at about three forty-five A.M. Speakin' of that, I'm tired."

"You oughta be," Earl said, a modicum of respect in his voice for the first time since at the crime scene.

"But I gotta get a line on some of these other people before I hit the rack. We gumshoes like to take weekends off, ya know, so I can suffer through today if I can line up some interviews for Monday. How 'bout lettin' me in the whereabouts of your people and givin' me a break, Earl?"

"I'm telling you the truth, Wally. I don't mind saying that I would rather talk to Bonnie and Margo and even Erin before you do, but if I knew where they were right now, I'd tell you."

Festschrift squinted at his old friend as if to size him up, then nodded. "One thing you never did was lie to me," he said. "Will you let me know when you find 'em?"

"Yeah, I will," Earl said, standing, as if to signal that the party was over. Festschrift didn't move.

"And will you let me talk to them first?"

"I can't promise that," Earl said.

"You don't want to obstruct justice, do ya, Earl?"

"That's another thing I've never done, Sergeant," Earl said evenly.

Wally cocked his head and raised his eyebrows, nodding agreement as if to silently apologize. "But you're not conducting an investigation, are you?" he said.

"Of course I am. Two of these people work for me and the other is very close."

"But you're not representing any of them, and you can't protect them the way their lawyers can."

"I wouldn't want to protect anyone I thought had murdered someone, but yes, I am representing Bonnie

Murray. You wanna see her file? She engaged me to put her son-in-law under surveillance on a domestic matter."

"No you don't, Earl," Festschrift said, exasperated. "This ain't no domestic case now. Anyway, everybody knows you don't take domestic cases. And besides, if you were watchin' *Mr.* Gibbons, you had the wrong party."

"We learned that," Earl said. "And I took this domestic case because Bonnie's a friend."

"She's also my prime suspect."

"And if I can prove that she came straight home from the gymnastics meet with Margo Franklin, will you let her off the hook?"

"Of course, depending on the trustworthiness of this Margo Franklin, who I would also like to meet soon."

Festschrift was startled when the three of us burst into laughter. "Sorry, Wally," Earl said. "but documenting the character of Margo Franklin will be the easiest job you've ever had."

"I could use an easy job."

The phone rang. "Yes," Earl said, "he is."

"Yeah, this is Festschrift. Uh-huh, yeah, give it to me." He motioned frantically for his notepad and pen. I scooped them up and delivered them to him, noticing the inscription on the barrel of the ballpoint: *Stolen from Harry's Union 76*.

Earl paced with his hands in his pocket while Festschrift scribbled. "A razor, huh? Yeah. Interesting. Yeah? I don't know. Let me know when you find out."

Wally hung up and folded his notepad, stuffing it into his shirt pocket. "Craziest thing," he said, wanting us to beg for information. None of us would. "All these hot-shot scientists workin' on the dumb thing, and a secretary winds up recognizing the murder weapon." He paused again, but we just waited. "It's a broken off piece of a lady's shaver, the cutting end of one of those disposable jobs."

"How do you know it's a lady's?" I asked, accusingly.

"'Cuz it's purple, boy," he said, smiling. "Would you shave wit' a purple razor?" Earl and Larry laughed. "They're checking on the brand now to find out where it might have been bought. That could help us a lot."

I wasn't sure I wanted to know all that that might tell us. I didn't want the murder weapon to be so femininely identified. And I suddenly felt the need to get the sleep I never really caught up on from the pre-dawn trip south. It wasn't to be, though. Margo was trotting up the stairs.

"Margo, where have you been?" Earl said.

"Oh, you're Margo," Wally said before she could answer. He extended his hand.

"Yes, Margo Franklin. And you're—?"

"Wally Festschrift. Chicago Homicide."

"Margo," Earl jumped in, "did you and Bonnie bring Erin home with you last night after the meet like you planned, and did Larisa come with you?"

Margo looked at Festschrift and back at Earl. "Well, no, Larisa wasn't coming with us, anyway, but as it turned out, I drove home alone."

"How did Mrs. Murray get home?" Wally asked.

"I'm not sure she went home. She said something about attending to some business and then going with

53

Chapter Five

"I'm sure your boss will be more than happy to fill you in on what's happened, Miss Franklin," Festschrift said, "but I have jurisdiction in this case and I have a few questions for you, if you don't mind."

"*I* mind," Earl said.

"I asked her if she minded, Earl, not you."

"You're in my office, Sergeant, and I'd rather you not conduct your business here."

"Earl, please," Margo said, "has something happened to Bonnie?"

"No. Johnny Bizell was murdered, and Sergeant Festschrift here—"

"I can speak for myself, if you don't mind." Wally briefed Margo on the case. "Tell me, Margo—may I call you Margo?—tell me, did Mrs. Murray ever say anything that would lead you to believe that she had an interest in harming Mr. Bizell?"

Margo was stunned. She stared past Festschrift and out the window, her hand drawn up to her mouth. "Oh, no—" she said quietly.

"I didn't get that, ma'am," Festschrift said politely. "Are you saying, no she didn't, or are you saying, oh no, because you recall that she did?"

"Of course she had a motive," Margo said absently.

"Of course she did. But did she ever say anything about acting on it?"

Margo looked desperately to Earl and then to me. We both shook our heads.

"Don't make it difficult for both of us, Miss Franklin. I know you spend a lot of time with Mrs. Murray, and I'm sympathetic to her distaste for a man she believes broke up her daughter's marriage. It's not illogical that she might have said something threatening, and it's not necessarily incriminating, either." I was amazed at how articulate Wally could be when he wasn't playing his illiterate cop routine.

Margo slumped into a chair, and Festschrift leaned back against a desk, directly in front of her. "Well, Earl," she said, "you may hate me for telling this, but Bonnie has been saying daily for weeks that she would kill Bizell if Greg and Linda's divorce ever became final. But it never did. In fact, Linda has not been seeing Johnny for a month. Bonnie, *and* Linda for that matter, have been optimistic about a reconciliation."

"But she said she would kill him?" Wally pressed.

"She didn't mean it! It's something you say when someone messes up your world or harms your children, and that's what happened."

"She may not have meant it," Festschrift said, scribbling madly again, "but somebody did it for her."

"You're saying she paid someone to do it?"

"I'm not saying anything except that her wish came true. Anybody here got anything more for me?" He buttoned up his coat. We said nothing. "Where can I find Mrs. Murray, if not at home?"

"I have no idea," Margo said. "I thought they'd be at either her place or Linda's."

"Why don't you try 'em on the phone one more time," Festschrift suggested. Margo looked like it was the last thing she wanted to do.

"Why don't *you*?" Earl said, but when Wally reached for a phone, Earl added, "on your own phone."

Festschrift straightened up, stuffed his notepad and pencil in his coat pockets, and left his hands there too. "So, the lines are drawn, huh, Earl? We're not gonna help each other on this?"

"Apparently not," Earl said. "It's not like you to be so eager to pin a murder on the first suspect you come up with, but that's where you're heading and I won't be part of it."

Festschrift turned his back and walked to the door. Without turning around, he said, "Just be sure of two things, Earl. Don't be guilty of the opposite, protecting extremely viable suspects. And don't obstruct justice by harboring criminals, witnesses, or suspects."

Earl stepped to the window and watched the detective pull away, heading the opposite direction from Bonnie's apartment. "Try Bonnie on the phone," he told Margo. "Fast."

As she dialed, Earl dictated the priorities to Larry and me. "Either of you on cases that can't be shelved for a few days?" We shook our heads. "Our top priority is to locate Bonnie and Linda and Erin. Festschrift hasn't even thought about Larisa yet, but she's so far removed from the situation that he may not even want to question her. Let's do whatever we have to do."

"Bonnie!" Margo said. "I've been trying to reach you! Have you heard what's happened. Yes, yes! Where are—"

Earl grabbed the phone. "Bonnie, listen," he said, "don't answer the phone. Just pack a few things and come over here as soon as you can. We'll talk then. Yes, I know. They aren't? You can't? Well, where could they—? Never mind for now, just hurry."

He hung up and spun around. "Larry, I want you to get over to Linda Gibbons's place and watch for her. Bonnie doesn't know where she and Erin are. You'll have an advantage over the cops who will also be staking out the place because you know what Linda and Erin look like. You have to get to them before Festschrift does."

As Larry bounded down the steps, Earl told me to arrange for a double room at the Holiday Inn in Northbrook just off the Edens "close enough to us, but just that much farther from downtown. Make it in Larry's name; I think his was the only one Wally didn't hear."

I was still on the phone when Bonnie drove up. "That was quick, Bonnie," Earl told her. "Good work. We're on our way to Northbrook. You can leave your car here."

Margo and Earl and Bonnie and I piled into Margo's car, Earl dragging his big white chart with him. As Margo blasted up the Edens, Earl questioned Bonnie. "I gotta know where you were and what happened last night," he said.

"Well, after the meet I had arranged to chat for a minute with Erin's coach, the guy with the funny name."

"Nik Adamski."

"Right, Nik. I told him that I was prepared to finance Erin's training this summer if he could give her individualized coaching when she returned from the European tour. That's been the dream of her life. He told me that it wouldn't be necessary because he had already been promised a grant by the US Olympic Committee and that both she and Larisa had qualified to train under the grant. Then I told him that things were looking better for Linda since Johnny had dropped her."

"You told him *that*?" Earl said, incredulous.

"Of course. Nik and all the girls know that story from way back," Bonnie said. "It's no news. He said it was important that they all encourage Erin during this difficult time."

"So what *is* the story with Linda and Greg? Are they getting back together? Did this Bizell really dump her?"

"Yes, he dumped her, and much as I hate to admit it, she loved him and it hurt her. She hated him for it, because she said she had been willing to break up her family for him. She's still kicking herself over that and says she couldn't blame Greg if he never forgave her, but she wants him back and will do anything to see that it happens."

"Meaning what?"

"Take all the blame, admit she was wrong, beg his forgiveness, whatever. She told me that while their relationship, hers and Greg's, had deteriorated over the years, he really did nothing that justified her affair. But the fact remains that she did fall for Bizell and she virtually gave up her husband for him, and then he dumped her."

"How did she take it?"

"Not well at first. She tried to get back at Johnny."

"Did she ever threaten him?"

"Oh, I'm sure she did."

Earl hung his head. "Did you ever hear her threaten him on the phone or anything?"

"No, only to me."

"She told you she had plans for him?"

"She only told me that, wrong as she was to have made the decision, there was no way she could let him get away with leaving her when she left her husband for him."

"C'mon, Bonnie, was she ever specific? Did she hate him enough to kill him for it?"

Bonnie bit her lip and looked away from Earl, watching the Saturday morning traffic on the expressway. "Where're we going?" she asked.

"To jail if you can't tell me more, Bon," Earl said gently.

"I don't want Linda to go to jail," she said, fighting tears. "I'd go first."

"You might." Earl told her about the involvement of Chicago Homicide and the fact that Margo had no choice but to repeat some of the things Bonnie had said about Bizell.

"Margo, how could you?" Bonnie said. "You know I was just raving as any mother would do! You would have said the same things. Yes, I hated Johnny Bizell enough to kill him, but you didn't hear me say that stuff for long after Linda admitted that she was as much to blame and that she'd made a conscious decision to break up her family for the creep. I nearly cheered for him when he dumped her."

"Bonnie, what could I do?" Margo said. "I was asked point blank if you had ever said you wanted to kill Johnny Bizell. You can't deny you said it many times, and I couldn't deny you said it, either."

"Don't blame Margo, Bonnie," Earl said. "What I want to know is whether Linda ever said the same things."

"Of course she did," Bonnie admitted.

Earl took Bonnie's hand. She was twenty years his senior, but he talked to her as if she was his daughter. "You know I love you, don't you, Bonnie?" She nodded. "You also know I have to ask you some hard questions, don't you?" She nodded again. "I'm going to ask them now, and when we have you and Margo settled in your hotel room, I'm going to want your answers. You must tell me the truth, Bonnie. I won't be the only person who asks, so be straight with me and we'll put everything we've got behind protecting you."

Margo exited at Lake-Cook Road and headed west to the light at Old Skokie Road/Route 41.

"Did you murder Johnny Bizell last night? Did you see him last night? Did Linda murder him? Did she see him?"

Margo turned left twice and then right into the parking

lot of the Inn. Once in the room, the four of us sat on the edges of the beds. Bonnie was crying. "It's time to talk to me, Bon," Earl said gently.

"I know," she said, holding a tissue to her face. Margo put her arm around the woman. "I didn't murder Johnny Bizell, much as I would have liked to have the courage. Yes, I saw him last night. When Linda joined Margo and me in the stands, she pointed him out to me."

"I didn't know that," Margo said, dropping her arm.

"I know, honey," Bonnie said. "We didn't want you upset about it."

"Upset?"

"Anyway, that's when we decided to change our plans. Erin and I were going to stay at my place, but I wanted to talk to Linda and be with her in case Johnny wanted to cause trouble. We couldn't imagine what he would be doing there after having not seen Linda for a month. What was worse, Greg had phoned Linda just before she left for the meet and told her that he might be there near the end himself and that he would try to greet her if he could. It was as encouraging as he'd been since Linda and Johnny broke up. She was excited about it like a first date, but she didn't see Greg and when Erin won the all-around, there was too much pandemonium and we didn't even look for him."

"Bonnie," Earl said, "were you with Linda every minute then until you picked up Erin and went home?"

"No."

"Where did she go, and for how long?"

"She told me to wait for Erin and bring her to the car.

She didn't know I was going to talk to Nik anyway, but she wanted to look for Greg at the exits and in the parking lot, so she said she would wait in the car."

"So how long were you apart?"

"Maybe twenty-five minutes," Bonnie said.

"Ouch."

Bonnie hid her face in her hands. "I know," she said. "It crossed my mind, too."

"When did it first cross your mind?"

"This morning when Erin came running in with the news. She had gotten up early to watch the news on TV to see if she would be on."

"How did Erin react?"

"She was just shocked. Not remorseful, just stunned."

"And Linda?"

"She burst into tears. She had, after all, loved the man, if only for a short time. I came home to get some things so I could stay with them a while longer, but when I called there before leaving my place again, there was no answer. I took Linda's car, so I have no idea where they are."

Earl shook his head. "Are you ready for one more tough one?" he asked.

"No, but go ahead."

"Are you fairly certain that Erin was in the locker room the whole time you talked to Nik and the rest of the time you waited for her?"

Bonnie stood as quickly as a matronly woman in her late fifties could stand. "No, you don't, Earl," she said, pacing and pointing at him, unable to restrain her tears. "Don't you dare cast aspersions on that child."

"I'm sorry, Bonnie, but I have to ask you if Erin ever said anything threatening about Johnny Bizell."

"No, you don't have to ask. Earl, you are talking about a thirteen-year-old child!"

"Fourteen," Margo corrected.

"Whatever! How dare you ask such a question?"

"Bonnie, why does it upset you so? Don't you know that my whole point is to establish alibis for all of you? I can't manufacture them, and I wouldn't."

"And I wouldn't expect you to! Don't you believe me, Earl?"

"Of course I do, but I have to know where Erin was between the time the meet ended, the interviews were over, and you picked her up outside the locker room door."

Bonnie went into the bathroom and shut the door, sobbing loudly.

"What are you after, Earl?" Margo asked.

"I'm not sure. I just don't like the way she exploded when I asked about Erin. I wasn't after anything when I brought it up. I was just trying to cover all the bases. But now I wonder if she's being straight with me."

"Do you believe her about not leaving the field house until she went to the car?"

"Oh, yes. I don't think Bonnie could have murdered Bizell. I don't even think she would have confronted him, though she might surprise me on that."

Bonnie returned. "So are we done, Earl? Is Margo going to stay with me until this thing is over, and are you going to protect me from having to answer questions from the press and the police?"

"I don't know, Bonnie. I can protect you from the press but not the police forever. And anyway, I don't think you're being fair with me."

"You're accusing me of lying?"

"I didn't say that. I have to know that you and Erin went directly to Linda's car when Erin came out of the locker room."

Bonnie fidgeted. "I lied to you, Earl, and I'm sorry, but you must believe me, it was only on one minor detail. I know you're trying to help, so I want you to believe me when I say that I am going to straighten out that lie and that I won't lie to you again."

"Of course."

"I waited longer than twenty-five minutes for Erin. It must have been closer to twice that. I spent the first fifteen or twenty minutes with the coach. Then I waited about half an hour until Larisa came out of the locker room. Other girls had been filing out and meeting their families, but Larisa recognized me and said that Erin had left earlier. She said she had skipped her shower and had ducked out to avoid the press. I ran out to Linda's car, and Erin was already there. I was going to scold her, but Linda said she had thought it would be better if she didn't leave Erin alone in the car, and she didn't want Erin running into more newsmen by going back in after me."

"How long had Linda waited in the car before Erin showed up?"

"It was the other way around. Erin waited outside the locked car for awhile with her parka hood up so no one would recognize her. Linda had looked around quite a while for Greg before giving up. I hope Larisa found her mother."

Earl looked depressed, deep in thought. "Huh? What? Found her mother?"

"Yes, she asked if I had seen her mother. She said her mother was going to meet her but that she hadn't appeared yet. I told her I didn't think I would know her mother if I saw her, and she said she would be the one with two bratty nine-year-olds fighting with her."

Earl took me into a corner to talk quietly. "I want you to go out and find a pay phone," he said. "Call Festschrift and tell him that I will personally apologize about my actions today and am willing to help all I can, but that I want the report on any fingerprints they may have found on Bizell's car."

"So, what do you think, Earl?" Bonnie was saying as I pulled on my coat.

"Well, I don't like it much," he said.

"What don't you like?"

"I don't like the fact that of all the people I've ever even heard of who were at that meet last night, I can't think of one, except maybe the coach, who has an alibi. I suppose the other girls on the team can vouch for Larisa up until the time she left the locker room, and maybe the ones who came out while you were waiting can vouch for you, but unless they knew you, you might have blended into the crowd. I don't even have an alibi for the Cumiskey twins, let alone their mother. Where was the father? Where was Linda? Where was Erin?"

"I just told you where *they* were," Bonnie reminded him.

"But an alibi, Bonnie, means someone can substantiate your whereabouts. Not even Margo is clean on that score."

Chapter Six

"Where's yer boss?" Festschrift wanted to know.

"Tied up at the moment," I said. "He just wanted me to ask for the information."

"What was your name again, kid?"

"Spence. Philip Spence."

"Yeah, right, Spence. Listen, why don't you come on down to the sixteenth precinct and learn a few things about the business?"

"I know a *few* things about the business," I said. "I've been in it a while myself."

"Yeah? You ever sit outside a lab waiting on some important piece of information, a hot bit of evidence?"

"Not exactly, but—"

"Well, then come on down. You know how to find us?"

"I think so."

"Good." *Click*.

A quick call to Earl brought permission and the insulting reminder to not proffer any of the information I had heard from Bonnie.

"I *know*, Earl," I said while driving him back to his Glencoe office in Margo's car.

"I suppose you do, Philip," he said. "Meet me back at the office later. I'll be trying to track down the missing gymnast and her mother. If you find out that Festschrift and Company have gotten to them already, call me immediately."

Festschrift was sitting on a wood bench in a grimy hallway outside the forensics lab when I approached. It was the only place he had looked at home since I had first seen him running the show in the parking lot of Proviso West High School. I didn't realize until I was upon him that he was dozing.

He sat with his ankles crossed—I guessed he hadn't crossed his legs at the knees for many moons. His top coat was buttoned, though champing at the gaps, and his hands were folded in front of his belly. His chin rested as close to his chest as possible. He made no noise, but his breathing was even and deep. I couldn't bring myself to wake him. He had been up as long as I had, but he hadn't had the luxury of trying to nap between dawn and noon as I had.

His face had grown dark with stubble, and he looked pitiable. I quietly sat at the other end of the bench and studied the man. He was good, Haymeyer had said. What drove him? Who was he, really? Why did he so love the work of tracking homicidal personalities even above getting ahead, making more money, gaining power? There was something pure about that.

And what about his bluster, his sarcasm, his earthiness? Was it just a show? Why the contempt for his former protégé and then boss? Was he just filling a role, or did he really resent Earl?

I determined to ask him. I also prayed that he would give me the right opening to talk about what I thought was important. I had regretted waiting for perfect opportunities before, and it wasn't going to happen again.

A door swung open from the lab and a white-coated and bespectacled woman emerged carrying a clipboard with a stack of forms on it. She leaned close to Festschrift's face and stooped to look into his eyes. She glanced at me. I held a finger to my lips and shook my head.

"You with him?" she mouthed. I nodded. She beckoned with a finger and I jumped up, almost too quickly. We walked down the hall and stood under a dim light over a washroom door. "You're on the Bizell case, right?" she asked. I couldn't lie.

"Yes," I said.

She began flipping pages. "You got all this weapon and wound stuff this morning, right?"

I nodded again as she kept turning pages and mumbling to herself, "Wound on left hand, blood type, carotid, jugular, uh-huh, yeah, yeah, yeah. You ever talk, uh—?"

"Name's Spence, Philip Spence. I'm sorry."

"You ever do more than nod and say your name and that you're sorry, Spence?"

"Uh, sure, sorry."

She looked at me, bemused. I was embarrassed and not unimpressed. She looked deep into my eyes and then back at her clipboard. "So you just want the new stuff, right?"

I nodded.

"There you go again," she said, smiling.

"I'm sorry," I said, knowing immediately that I had set myself up again. It isn't easy letting someone think you're something you're not.

"OK," I said, "uh, forgive me, but yes, I just want the new stuff, thank you."

She flashed the smile again and turned back to her papers. "OK, Mr. Spence, we have fingerprints from the driver's side, Bizell's only. On the passenger's side door and window we have what we think are prints from three different hands, two big ones and a small one. Our bets are on two men and a woman, but we don't want to rule out a young boy or a very small man, maybe a girl."

"Thank you."

"Sure. Will you give this stuff to Rip?"

"Rip?"

"Van Winkle?"

"Oh, yeah, sorry."

"How come you're so sorry, Spence? You like workin' Saturdays as much as I do?"

"Yeah, plus I feel guilty."

"Hm, I haven't heard this line before. Let's have it."

"It's not a line, ma'am, it's just that I let you think I was with Festschrift."

"Uh-oh," she said musically, raising her brows and taking back the clipboard.

"Oh, no, I don't mean I lied to you. I mean I am with Festschrift, but not in the way you think."

"Well, you're not dating him, are you? Who are you?"

"I gave you the right name. I'm with a private detective agency, and I *was* invited here by Sergeant Festschrift."

"But you're not supposed to have direct access to this file, are you?"

72

"No, ma'am, I'm afraid not."

"Forget the politeness, Spence. You just swindled me out of classified information."

"I'm sorry."

She swore. "I've already heard that one, remember?"

She stomped back down the hall to Festschrift and swatted him on the hands with her papers. "Here ya go, Sleepy. Can I go home now?"

"Huh? Oh, sure, Marilyn. Sorry you hadda come in. Take the rest of the day off."

"Everybody's sorry," she said. Festschrift looked puzzled, but I was grateful she hadn't told him what I'd done. She probably would later.

Festschrift shifted his weight and leaned toward the light, holding the papers close to his face and scrounging up a pair of half glasses with his free hand. He read each page carefully, all the fine print, then announced that there wasn't much of anything new but that he might have to begin fingerprinting everyone who had been at the gymnastics meet the night before. He looked so serious that it threw me. Then he let his head fall back and cut loose a belly laugh that echoed throughout the precinct headquarters. I smiled.

"So what's yer philosophy of life, Spence?" Festschrift said.

I was floored. "Pardon me?"

"I study death to make sense of life," he said. "You made sense of it yet?"

"I think maybe I have."

73

"Oh, yeah? One of the myths of youth. Seems we all know more about life the younger we get. Have you found that?"

"I guess I know what you mean," I said. "I mean, I do realize every day how little I know about everything there is to know."

"Yeah, me too," he said, staring off into space as if he was about to fall back to sleep. I didn't want to let it drop, but I had never heard of a way to segue from a question like he had just popped to a cogent argument for faith in God.

"Do you really wanna know my philosophy of life?" I asked.

"Not really, no," he said, smiling apologetically. "I ask that of a lot of people, just to see what they'll say. But, OK, go ahead, what would you have said if you had known what was coming?"

"Well, I'm a Christian," I said.

"Yeah, well, hey, we've got a few of those on the department. More than a few I should say. They've got some kinda lodge or club called Cops for Christ or somethin'. They come on a little strong, and I'm not in the mood right now, so I'll make a deal with ya. You save your sermon, and I'll buy you the best steak in town."

It was apparent he *wasn't* in the mood, and the offer sounded too good to pass up.

Festschrift's unmarked squad car looked and rode like the hand-me-down it was. With its blackwalled tires, whip antenna, spotlight, and city license plate, it screamed cop car louder than any Chicago blue and white with lights.

The ride was rough, the squeaks loud, the brakes metal on metal. It rolled on the curves and rocked at stoplights. Inside it looked like a cab with a couple of hundred thousand miles on it. Festschrift admitted to only 160 thousand plus.

He drove like an old lady on her way to church, which didn't seem to fit. I knew he was tired. We dined at a stuffy little place he called cozy. In reality, it reminded me of the inside of his car, decorated in Early Akron. He appeared a connoisseur of good food, however, and in that I was not disappointed.

We sat in vinyl covered kitchen-type chairs at a square formica table on linoleum floors and were waited on by men who understood so little English that we had to point out our entrees on the menu. "Plenty of it and plenty good," the sergeant said. And he was right.

He was greeted by a half dozen or so patrons as the night wore on. "I eat here often," he said simply. He'd identify the acquaintances by precincts. "The old lady left me goin' on four years ago," he said, always with his mouth full. "We'd been together, if you can call it that, sixteen years and had four boys, every one of 'em a bum. I even got one behind bars right now."

I didn't know what to say. "I never had time for her or them," he said. "It's my own fault and I know it, but then my old man never had time for me and I turned out awright, didn't I?"

I wasn't sure exactly how he'd turned out, with four no account sons and a divorce.

"I still see her around. She's OK. I don't blame her. I'm no prize. I love the job more than anything or anybody, and I can't change that. But I don't hate her, and she takes a big chunk of my check every two weeks, so we might's well be on speakin' terms."

"Why do you love the job so much?" I had to ask. He didn't seem like such a sensitive, loving, humanity-oriented person.

"I'm a justice nut. I like the puzzles, the mystery. Every homicide is different, ya know. Like this one. I got me an idea on this one that's kinda bizarre, and I'll trade you secrets if you want. I know you know something 'cuz my guess is ol' Earl has found one of the women I'm looking for. Wanna trade?"

"I don't know. I don't think so."

"You just tol' me something, you know that?"

"No. What'd I tell you?"

"You tol' me I was right. You told me that Earl found one of 'em at least. You're deciding not to tell me what you learned, but you *did* learn something just like I said."

I cocked my head. He had me. "But I really can't say anything," I said.

"No, 'course you can't, and I can't bully Earl with my obstruction-of-justice routine either. He knows that. These women aren't wanted yet, so he's not harboring anything."

Wally ordered a carafe of wine, offered me some, then drank the whole thing over the next forty-five minutes with no apparent effect on his mind or speech. This was a man used to eating and drinking heartily, and then, in a succession I wouldn't have guessed, he decided he was ready for dessert. "I never drink on duty," he said. "And I'm takin' tomorrow off. That oughta give Hayseed a real jump on me, but I'll get to all the people eventually whether he sees 'em first or not."

He busied himself with his deep dish apple pie and what appeared to be a pint of ice cream.

"Tell me something," I said. "Have you ruled out any mob connection in this murder?"

He gestured and tried to talk, even with his mouth jammed as never before, as if I had come up with an idea so ludicrous, so obviously in left field that he couldn't let rebuttal wait until he had swallowed. "Oh, no, small time, small time. In fact, if Bizell had been snuffed two days from now, I wouldn't have had the honor of handling it. The vice control division thought he was tighter with some south suburban mobsters, but all he was into was some porn and some dope. He had no real connections. They just trailed him a little and found that he was nothing but a super salesman type, number one in his company, who liked to run in some fast circles. But he was all show. Some of our informants told us he was too loud for their tastes. They like to play it close to the vest, you understand, and you don't do that with his golden mane and that hot silver 'Vette o' his. He found himself uninvited to the kinds of gatherings we like to keep an eye on."

"But they were still watching him at the time he was murdered?"

"Just barely. They knew he was home much of the evening and then went to that gymnastics meet. They didn't expect much there, so they left him. It might have been the last tail of him anyway, so when the call hit ISPERN, one of our guys recognized the name and called VCD. Then it fell to me."

"ISPERN and VCD?"

"Illinois State Police Emergency Radio Network and Vice Control Division. Anyways, Bizell was strictly a small time womanizer with a few bucks, fewer friends, and hardly any family to speak of. This sucker gon' be buried without much fanfare."

"Sad."

"Think so, huh? Wait 'til you been in the business as long as I have. Like I tol' ya, I'm a justice freak. People have to pay for what they do. I was a lousy husband and father, and I don't like the price, but I'm payin' it. I'm a good cop, and I earn the rewards for that. It's fair. Sad because a creep like Bizell buys it? Not me. But whoever did it has to pay, regardless of the reason."

"And you've got a bizarre idea about this one?"

"Yeah, but you're not in the market for a trade, am I right?"

"You're right."

"Ah, who cares? I got nothin' to lose. If I'm right, Earl can't protect her anyway."

"I know you think Bonnie did it, but that's not so bizarre. I don't think she did, but she sure had a motive."

"Nah, I'm past that. I haven't totally ruled her out, you understand. One of the things I like about this work is that

78

I often come back to someone I've eliminated early. It's all part of the game. Anyway, I'm thinking gymnast."

"Gymnast? Erin?"

"Gymnast, yes, Erin, I don't know. She might be a little small. I'm guessing whoever did it leaned in the window on the driver's side, reached around behind Bizell's head with the right hand, and did the damage quickly. But it had to be someone that Bizell didn't fear. He had to think of the gesture as affectionate or a greeting or not know what it was to let someone do that. He probably never saw the murder weapon; it would have been tucked into the hand. A little girl might have arms long enough to pull that off, but I don't know."

"But why a gymnast, and if a gymnast, why not Erin, who has a motive just like her grandmother does?"

"A gymnast because I studied up a little at the library early this afternoon and I learned that those little beauties develop incredible muscles in their hands. They can grip and squeeze and take punishment. They have hand strength like grown men, and that's what it would take to have inflicted this wound so successfully. Grown women anyway."

"But you're not thinking of Erin?"

"Oh, I s'pose if I knew more, I might think Erin. But I say I'm not thinking of her only because I really have nothing to go on. I need to chart the comings and goings of everyone at the meet who might have had a motive. The way Earl was doing in your office today."

"You learn that from him?" I asked.

"You kiddin'? He learned it from me. Ask him."

79

"You like Earl?"

"Love him." He said it without a moment's hesitation.

"You mean it."

"You bet I do. He's one of the best I've ever seen, straight as an arrow. My kind of a guy."

"You don't act like that around him."

"You think I want him to know? A guy's gotta keep some advantage. Don't you?"

"I don't know. Nah."

"That's *your* advantage."

"Pardon?"

"That self-effacing bit of yours. You gotta be good or Earl wouldn't waste his time with you, but you pull that Columbo, poor-dumb-me act and I'm guessing you're dumb like a fox. Am I right?"

I was embarrassed. Flattered. I shrugged.

"See?" he said. "I was right."

A beeper went off in his pocket and he nearly had to stand to get his bulk out of the way so he could reach it. He clicked it off and headed for the phone. On the way he passed the waiter who had our check. "Jes' put it on the cuff, Georgio," Wally said, "and t'row in a fifteen percenter for yourself, huh?"

"Earl put your cohort on the Gibbons residence today, huh?" Wally said when he returned.

It was apparent he already knew, so I didn't feel I was breaking any confidence by nodding.

"Well, he blew it. We got to Linda Gibbons before he did, and when he appeared, she identified him as someone

80

she had seen before. She said he was a maintenance man she had seen once in the building. He once walked in on her and Johnny Bizell. You wanna go see him?"

"Where is he?"

"We busted him. Had to. He's in the slam at the nineteenth precinct station. Not far from here. You can bail him out if he's got an alibi."

Chapter Seven

I called Earl on the way out of the restaurant, and he was none too thrilled that I had let so much time elapse before contacting him. I didn't want to tell him that I actually found his old nemesis fascinating.

"Well, you told me to call you if I found that Chicago had found Linda and Erin before Larry had. And they have."

"You're not doing your homework, Philip."

"What do you mean?"

"You're giving me second-hand information."

"Well, sure I am, but it's what Wally Festschrift said based on a phone call he just took."

"Did he actually tell you that *both* Linda and Erin were picked up?"

"I guess I just assumed—"

"Assumed is not homework. Call me from the nineteenth and I'll tell you where *we* have Erin."

In the car I asked Festschrift how they happened to find Linda without finding Erin.

"We just staked out the apartment, saw a little too much of your buddy there, what's his name?"

"Larry Shipman."

"Yeah, and when we saw him approach a young

woman, we moved in. The woman was Linda Gibbons, she was on foot, and she still hasn't told us where she dumped Erin."

Linda had agreed to questioning at the precinct house, but no charges had been filed and she was free to go. She had not contacted a lawyer, and from what she told the police, it was apparent she didn't need one. Not that she had an alibi; she didn't. She just told them very little.

She said she had left the gymnastics meet alone to look for her estranged husband at the exits and in the parking lot. When she was unsuccessful she headed for her car because it was locked, and she didn't want her mother and her daughter to get out there first and have to wait for her. As it was, her daughter was already waiting for her and her mother came along some time later. The story was so much like Bonnie's version that it was eerie. It could have been the truth, or it could have been tailor-made.

Festschrift asked her where she had been when he had looked for her that morning.

"My mother went home in my car to get some things so she could stay with us longer, but a few minutes after she left I had this fear that the press would somehow put it all together and try to badger Erin about it. We just threw some things together and jumped on a bus, but I'd rather not say where we went. Anyway, she's there now."

"It shouldn't be hard to guess," Wally said. "I'd say she's either with her coach or with her friend Larisa."

Linda stiffened, but Festschrift didn't pursue it. "The time will come when we need to talk to her, Mrs. Gibbons."

She nodded. "I know. But not yet."

A desk clerk approached. "There's a Mr. Hayworth on the phone for you, Sergeant."

"Haymeyer?"

"Oh, yessir, that was it."

"I don't remember your name, but I know you work in Mother's office," Linda said. "You've been at some of the meets."

"Yeah, quite a few of them actually. I'm Philip."

"Oh, yes, Philip Spence. You used to go with Margo."

"Yeah."

"You must think I'm a terrible person, Philip."

"Oh, no, well I, uh—"

"You do, and you're right. I am. But I hope you don't think I'm so low that you can't give me a ride home—" and she leaned close to whisper "—or to see Erin when I leave here. I'd rather not have to ride back the way I came, with the cops."

"Sure. I don't blame you, but you'll have to ride with Sergeant Festschrift as far as the sixteenth precinct where my car is."

She nodded as Festschrift returned. "Well, I'm gonna let your comrade go," he announced.

"Larry? Why?"

"That was Earl. He said you guys were at the Sox-Yankees game last night."

"I could have told you that," I said.

"Well, good, I've got two unimpeachable sources."

Linda was puzzled. "So I *had* seen that guy before? I remembered him from the time he walked in on Johnny

85

and me, but he's with Earl too, huh? What was the maintenance man bit all about?"

"That was back when your mother thought *you* were the innocent party, and she was trying to get Greg in trouble."

She fell silent.

"We'll likely want to be talking to you again soon," Festschrift told Linda as Larry entered. "Stay accessible."

She didn't respond.

"I haven't seen so many lowlifes in a cell since high school biology," Larry said, eager to get going. "Philip, can you take me to my car up there in Linda's neighborhood?"

"Sure! I mean, that is, if it's all right with you, Linda, that Larry goes along. Is it?"

She shrugged. "Make it a party," she said.

Festschrift dropped us off at my car and said he was going home for some sleep. I was the last to slide out of his car and he grabbed my wrist. "Lemme tell ya something, kid," he said. "I like you, so I'm gonna let you in on one more thing we found at the scene. I'll only tell ya if you assure me we're after the same thing here: justice."

I nodded.

"Perfume," he said.

"Perfume?"

"Perfume. It has different ingredients than men's cologne and the like. On the back of the collar of the dead man and a little on the back of his neck, there were traces of the elements in perfume. When the lab beefed it up by adding to each element and mixing, they matched the smell of a brand name fragrance. Experts—that is, the women in forensics and a few secretaries, not to mention the girls behind the cosmetics counter at Carson's down the street—agree unanimously. It's something they call Chantilly. Ever heard of it?"

"No."

"Well, you've probably smelled it. I recognized it. Not real common, but something you remember." He pulled a heat-sealed plastic packet from his pocket. "Take this," he said. "Take a whiff when you get a chance. And if you smell it on any of our suspects, let me know. You owe me one."

I knew at least *that* was true. "Get some sleep," I said.

"Don't worry, I'll probably be asleep before I get out of the car."

"And thanks for dinner."

"Don't mention it, and hey, keep your advantage."

I knew what he meant, but I pretended I didn't.

Speaking of pretending, Larry put his head against the window and pretended to sleep as the three of us rode to the north side and Linda's apartment. But with Linda in the mood for talking to someone who couldn't put her away for murder, I was sure Larry didn't miss a syllable.

"Since we're all adults here and there's no hiding it from you guys, you wanna know what the toughest thing is for a woman who's had an affair she regrets?"

"I admit it wasn't the first thing on my mind this morning," I said, "but, sure, I'll listen."

"It 's that you get put in a bag. Compartmentalized. I'm an average woman. I had always been a faithful wife. I worked. I was a good housekeeper and a good mother. But I met a guy from my husband's office, and something happened. I was bored with my life and here was a gorgeous guy who paid attention to me. I fell in love with him.

"It was wrong. He was wrong; I know that now more clearly than ever. And I regret it, but do you think I'll be able to erase it from my life? Never. Even if Johnny hadn't been killed, I never would have really been forgiven. I can even see it in *your* eyes. An edge has been taken off. I'm seen as worse than just someone who has made one mistake. By people who know, I will never be considered worthy of normal status again. Am I right?"

I didn't know what to say. Of course she was right. She was even right about how I viewed her. "I'm in no position to condemn you," I said.

"Well, that's nice. Maybe you've made a mistake or two in your life too, huh?"

I didn't exactly want to put myself in her category, and there I went, doing just what she predicted, categorizing her. I couldn't stop the next line from coming out of my mouth. "Well, not that kind of a mistake, no. But, yes, I have made some serious mistakes. Why do you think I'm no longer engaged to Margo?"

"I couldn't tell you. I don't know her well, but from what I can tell, you should have hung on to that one. But anyway, did you just hear yourself? You've made some mistakes but nothing as horrible as mine."

"I didn't—"

"I know you didn't say that or mean to imply it, but it's what you think, and I can't blame you. I used to react the same way. I thought the only people who could cheat on their husbands or wives had to be disgusting wanton types. I'm telling you, it happened to me, a normal person, but I'll never be normal again. The worst part is, my husband looks at me and talks to me and treats me the same as everyone else does. Something has been damaged, and no matter what I do, I won't be able to fix it."

I was more than bewildered by this woman unburdening herself to me when I was just this side of being a total stranger. She must have been implying by that openness that she couldn't even say these things to her mother because her mother was as guilty as the rest of us. And why do I say guilty? Are *we* guilty? *Is* there something wrong with seeing someone in a different light who has nearly ruined the lives of everyone around them by their behavior? Or *were* we unfair, especially now that she was admitting it and not blaming her husband or her lover?

"Greg and Erin and I will probably have to move away to escape this reputation," she said quietly, defeatedly. "That is if he'll ever have me again."

I wanted to tell her that of course, he'd take her back, but I didn't even know the man. I wanted to change the subject, to ask her about perfume, anything. But talking about something else would merely tell her that I didn't care about her problem. And, strangely, I did. I don't know why; I guess she just reached me with her argument.

I knew the right thing to tell her was that there was Someone who could forgive her, Someone who understood, Someone who had experience with people who had sinned and wanted forgiveness, in fact, even with women who had committed adultery. But with Larry in the backseat, pretending to sleep so as to avoid commenting on her treatise, I wasn't ready to hit her with it.

"How did you feel about Johnny's death?" I asked.

"I cried."

"I know, but how did you feel? Sad? Angry? Guilty?" I knew I shouldn't have said that.

"Guilty? Hardly. You think I killed him, don't you?"

"No, I—"

"You *do*!"

"No I don't. I meant that it's very likely that whoever killed him thought they were doing you a favor. Therefore if you didn't kill him, you still might feel responsible for the fact that someone did."

"The only person responsible for Johnny's death was Johnny. The way he chewed me up and spit me out qualified him for getting what he deserved. No, I didn't do it. And I wasn't angry or sad. Shocked is the better word. I had been in love with him, or at least I thought I had. I've never lost anyone close to me except my own father, and that's been a long time ago, and he had been sick quite a while. I could accept that. This was horrible. The thought of someone I had known intimately being murdered—" She shuddered.

I parked at the curb, not far from where I had seen

Johnny Bizell's car several times. As soon as I shut off the engine, Larry came to and headed out the back door. Before shutting it he leaned back in, touched Linda on the shoulder, and said, "A piece of advice to take or leave: Forget what people think. Only you know what's inside, and that's all that matters. See ya," and he slammed the door and trotted to his own car.

"Oh," she said softly, as if she had been wounded by the perfection of his words. I sat there wishing I had said them. "That was sweet," she added.

I decided that if she had been any woman other than one who had been willing to let her family fly apart, I would have treated her like a lady. "Hang on a second, and let me get the door for you," I said.

I ran around to her side and then walked her up to her apartment. She handed me the key, and I unlocked the door. "Can you come in for a minute?" she asked.

"No, I really shouldn't. I've got to call my boss."

"You can call him from here."

I hesitated.

"You're afraid of me, aren't you? You see? I'll never be able to be a normal person again."

"Let me tell you the truth, Mrs. Gibbons—Linda—I'd be afraid of Snow White if I were alone with her."

She laughed sympathetically. "I'll tell you what I'll do, Philip," she said. "I'll leave the door open, and I'll sit in the living room, and you can use the phone. But hurry, because I have to talk to Earl too. I need to see if he got a call from Coach Adamski—who is also afraid of me, I might add—and was able to pick up Erin from his home. I didn't know where else to take her; I didn't want to burden the Cumiskeys."

"I'll find out for you."

Earl asked that Linda get on the extension phone. He told us that Coach Adamski had reached him at the office shortly after I had dropped Earl off. "I picked her up at his place, and she's with Bonnie now."

"I want to see her," Linda said.

"You can, but we'll have to be careful. It's likely you're being watched, and you could lead the police right to Bonnie *and* Erin. Philip can bring you to the office where we can talk. When we are sure no one is tailing you, we can scoot you over to see them."

"Where are they?"

"I'd rather not say on the phone. How did things go downtown?"

"Not bad. I just told them my story, nothing that should clear me, I wouldn't think, but they fingerprinted me and let me go quickly."

"They fingerprinted you?"

"Yeah."

"Did they charge you with anything?"

"No."

"Were you informed of your rights?"

"Yes, but I thought it would be better if I didn't appear to be hiding anything."

"If they fingerprinted you it means they may have found prints on the car."

"They did, Earl," I said.

"Let's talk about it when you get here," Earl said.

On the way to the office, I asked Linda if she knew anyone who used Chantilly perfume. "Of course," she said, "Larisa has everyone on the team using it. Erin uses it when she gets some from Larisa or I can afford it."

"But Larisa started it?"

"I think so. Her mother swims in it. I can tell when she's coming or even when she's been somewhere. Why?"

"Just curious."

At the office, Earl told Linda that Bonnie and Margo and Erin were at the Northbrook Holiday Inn and that everyone was fine. "I know you've been asked a ton of questions, and Philip has filled me in on your version of what happened last night, but I need to get some more information from you if I can. Do you fear that someone you know and love might have killed Johnny Bizell?"

Linda lifted her chin and looked at the ceiling, catching a short breath and then exhaling. She closed her eyes and dropped her chin to her chest in a pose that reminded me how Festschrift had looked not so many hours earlier.

"Yes," she said, barely above a whisper. "I do."

"Who?"

"I don't know. Erin knew all about him but would never talk to me about it. I can't see her having done it, and I probably couldn't accept it even if she told me she had.

"My mother had the desire but not the drive. I don't think she could have done it, though she wanted to and

93

threatened to many times. When she got the whole story, I think she would have rather murdered me.

"It's my husband I worry about. He said he was going to be there, but I never saw him. I didn't expect to see Johnny, but I did. I don't know. I wish I knew where Erin and my mother were after the meet, and I'm sure they're wishing the same about me."

She was still staring at the floor. "The first several times Greg accused me of seeing Johnny, he blamed it all on Johnny. He couldn't see that I was as much at fault, because that threatened him too much. I don't know if he ever got past that blinded view of it. He probably still wants to blame it on Johnny, and I know he hated him enough to kill him. Whether he did or not, I couldn't say."

"Well, he's been virtually cleared by Sergeant Festschrift," Earl said.

"Oh?" Linda didn't appear fully relieved about that.

"Yeah. Seems he was with Ernest Cumiskey for a couple of hours immediately following the meet."

"Larisa's dad? What for?"

"Talking to him about a job with Cumiskey's company, I guess."

"No kidding? Greg has always admired Ernest. He's such a go-getter. Goes after only the best people. That says a lot about Greg. Had he been selling well lately in spite of all this, do you know? It doesn't seem likely. Even when we were happy and life was relatively normal, Greg was always just a little above average in the company as far as sales went. Maybe something else about Greg

94

impressed Mr. Cumiskey. Was he offered a job? Did he take it?"

"I have no idea," Earl said. "Excuse me."

He answered the phone and his face clouded. "I see, yes. Thanks, Wally. Yes, I will."

He replaced the receiver and walked deliberately to where Linda sat. She looked up at him expectantly. "I'm afraid I won't be able to take you to see Erin just now," he said. "I've been instructed by the police to hold you here for a few minutes until they arrive."

"What is it, Mr. Haymeyer?"

"Sergeant Festschrift left instructions that he was only to be awakened if anything important turned up. When your fingerprints matched those on the passenger door of Johnny Bizell's car, they thought it was important enough. And so do I."

Chapter Eight

Sure enough, we had been tailed to the office, and in just a few minutes, homicide detectives had entered, read Linda Gibbons her rights for the second time that day, and took her downtown to await arraignment on charges that she had murdered Johnny Bizell.

"I'm not ready to bring Bonnie out into the open yet," Earl said. "Maybe tomorrow or Monday." I could tell he was seething. "I don't know if Linda is guilty or not, but if she isn't, she has only herself to blame for our not being able to protect her. How could she have seen Bizell recently without telling even her mother?"

"Are you sure she didn't tell her mother?"

Earl got on the phone. "Yes, I know it's nearly midnight, Margo," he said, "and I'm sorry, but I must talk with Bonnie."

He told her that Linda would be charged with the murder because of the fingerprints, her motive, and her lack of an alibi, and he said he wanted Bonnie to hear it from him first. "It'll make the Sunday papers," he said.

Erin was sleeping, and Bonnie and Margo agreed not to tell her. "I'll come over there tomorrow morning and spend some time with you," Earl said.

"Tell Margo to be ready to bring your car back here and go to church with me," I said.

He told her. "She says she'll meet you at her church at nine-thirty." Oh well, it was worth a try.

I was exhausted, but I couldn't keep the wheels from turning as I undressed for bed. There was no way this investigation could be this cut and dried. No one had an alibi for Linda, and she had lied about not having seen Johnny except from across the field house. Apparently, she had been in or near his car.

But if she had murdered him, wouldn't she have been more concerned with convincing people—like Larry and me—of that rather than holding forth about the injustices meted out to fallen wives? In my mind, she had been truly concerned about how to overcome the consequences of her actions against her husband and her marriage, not actions against her former lover.

One thing I hadn't asked her and wished I had. I wanted to know if she had ever used her daughter's perfume. She said she only bought it when she could afford it or when Erin borrowed some, but did women use each other's perfume? I didn't know. I would ask Margo in the morning. That is, if I could get up early enough to meet her at her church at nine-thirty.

If I had known what I would be getting into, I probably wouldn't have made the effort.

I slept without moving for seven hours, rose, showered, dressed for church, went out for a paper and a roll and coffee, brought them back to my apartment, and sat eating and reading for an hour. It was hard to get past the front page when the banner headline screamed the news: MOTHER OF GYM STAR CHARGED.

If Erin could keep her equilibrium in the face of all this—I wondered if she would continue to compete. How could she? The most important meets of the year were approaching, but how could she be at her best? How could she even have her mind on her training? She was a fine-tuned machine. A lack of concentration at the level she performed would not only affect her score, but it would also be terribly dangerous. You don't just throw yourself at a balance beam four inches wide and four feet off the ground or fling your body around uneven parallel bars at breakneck speed without having 100 percent concentration.

Margo's church may have been small, a white clap-board structure that looked out of place in the sprawling North Shore, but it was crowded. I arrived early to watch for her but still had to park a block and a half away. I was strolling toward the front of the church when she arrived with a car full of kids who were still a few years shy of ten. She was shouting instructions to them, straightening their hair, making sure each had his or her Bible, tucking in shirts and blouses, and shouting, "I'll see you right here at noon, and no running!" They were all running.

"Hi, Philip," she said, still moving. "Good to see you. Listen, I have to make an announcement in each department and then lead a discussion group in our Sunday School class, so if you wait for me there I'll be a little late." She pointed the way down the stairs and past the washrooms, through the primary department and near the piano at the end of the fellowship hall, behind the partition. "That's where we meet."

"I'll find it," I said, but I had not looked when she had pointed. I just kept staring at her. She was radiant in dark blue with just the right accessories as usual. Energetic. Eager. Enthusiastic. She saw that I wasn't paying attention to her directions and stopped. "Philip," she scolded, blushing. She physically turned me around and pointed over my shoulder. "Down there," she said, "and left past all that stuff I just listed."

I turned and watched her hurry away. She stopped and ran back. "I forgot to tell you, our class breaks up early because the choir uses that piano to practice just before the service. And I'm in the choir, so save me a seat near the front, OK?"

I nodded. No wonder she liked this church better than the one we used to go to. She owned it, or at least she ran it. So many people greeted her that it was obvious she knew everyone and was a favorite.

I was the first to arrive at the partitioned off young adults class area near the piano, so I just sat and waited. The first few people didn't greet me, but after a bunch had arrived, I was asked to introduce myself. I just said my name and that I was with Margo Fr—and I could hardly get any more out amid the cacophony of *ohs* and *ahs* and *oh reallys* from the women and men alike.

"Are you going with her?" someone asked.

The others interrupted. "You shouldn't ask *that!*" some said, but they all waited for my answer.

I wanted to say that we used to be engaged and that we were sort of going together again, but we weren't, and she might not want people to know of her broken engagement, so I just said, "No, we work together."

When Margo arrived, she was again greeted by seemingly everyone, made her announcement, took a very active role in the discussion, and when we broke up into smaller groups, she led ours. I was ill with admiration for how she had blossomed, and painfully aware that it had been without my input. In fact, there was no way she could have emerged like this had we stayed together. No wonder she didn't appear to need me anymore. She had everyone else.

I would have gotten a kick out of it during the worship service if she had eyed me from the choir for a quick smile or even a wink, but I didn't get so much as a glance. She was into her work, concentrating, doing it right. I hadn't even been aware that she had an interest in singing, let alone ability.

After the service, I stood in the background while she chatted with dozens of different people, touching them, smiling, asking, working her magic, making them feel great. Men, women, the elderly, children, peers. She should have been running for office. I can't even say she neglected me. She introduced me often, pulling me next to her to meet people, telling them that I was a bright young investigator with an unlimited future, all that stuff. I wanted to believe it in the worst way.

I followed her to her car where she piled the kids in, turned on the radio, and then stood outside to talk with me. "I'm sorry I was so busy," she said. "But that's what

I like about this place. I think the problem I had for so long was that my faith was inactive, inward, stagnant. I enjoy exercising it, but I hope I didn't make you feel like a tagalong."

"Well, I felt that way, but it wasn't your fault, and I wouldn't have wanted it any other way. I just hope I wasn't in the way."

"Of course you weren't."

"Anyway, you'll have lunch with me, won't you?"

"Sure, why not? After I drop the kids off I'll take the car back to my apartment. You can pick me up there in a half hour. Dutch?"

"No, I'm buying, and I want you to know that it bothers me when I ask you out and you adjust it so it's a double date or a group or Dutch like we're merely co-workers."

She was embarrassed, and I was sorry I had gotten into it right then and there. She looked back toward the kids in the car who were climbing back and forth over the seat and eager to get home for dinner. "You're right, Philip, and I'm sorry. I accept your invitation for lunch, and I'll be ready when you arrive." And I finally got my wink. Now what was I going to do with a half hour when it only took ten minutes to drive to her apartment?

I went to the office, straightened my desk, walked down the hall to my apartment, searched for a section of the paper I hadn't read but couldn't find one, straightened my tie, ran a damp towel over my shoes, brushed my teeth, and headed out, still with time to kill.

I pulled into the parking lot at Margo's building at the same time she did. She jumped from the car, waved as she ran to the building, and was back in less than ten minutes. She had changed from her blue dress gathered at the waist to a sweater and slacks outfit in beige and tan, highlighted by tiny gold chains around her neck. "You look great," I said.

"Thanks. So do you. I suppose you know that Linda called Erin last night."

"You're kidding."

"Nope. She was given one phone call, and she called Erin. She was pretty crafty too, because the room was in Larry's name and she had to remember the name of everyone on our staff and ask if they were booked. She finally hit on Shipman and then rang the room. She told Erin that she wanted her not to worry or to feel too badly and that she had wanted her to hear it from her mother, not from anywhere else. She also told Erin that she was innocent and that she would be cleared, even though it looks bad now. Erin said her mother told her, 'If you know for sure, because I'm telling you, that I didn't do it, you can concentrate on your gymnastics and not let it affect your scores. I'll be rooting for you.'"

"Wow."

"I know."

"What do you think, Margo? Who killed Bizell?"

"You really want to know what I think? I think it's strange that of these three women, Bonnie, Linda, and Erin, each thinks either of the other two could have done it."

"That's true. Does that make it likely that one of them did?"

"Oh I don't think so, Philip. I mean I'm not sure that it

wasn't one of them; in fact, I'd lean more toward Linda right now with the fingerprints and all, but just because they fear the guilt of each other doesn't prove anything."

"I'm frankly a little wary of Greg Gibbons in this whole thing," I said.

"And don't leave out Larisa."

"Larisa?"

"Yes, Philip, I think Larry might have been onto something there when he first questioned that relationship. It may be because I never enjoyed one like it, but it *is* a little too good to be true. And either way, Larisa could have had a motive."

"Either way?"

"Whether she loves Erin or hates her for stealing her glory. If she really cares about Erin and wants her to be happy, she might have taken it upon herself to eliminate the problem in Erin's life. And if she has been phony all this time and really resents Erin, perhaps she murdered Bizell, hoping either that it would appear that Erin or her mother did it and would ruin her career."

"Bizarre."

"Not when women are involved. It could happen, Philip."

"That doesn't make it any less bizarre."

"Oh, this place is supposed to be neat," she said as I parked in front of a small French restaurant. "I hope we're done talking shop."

"Almost," I said, hoping the same thing. "I just need to know who in that gymnastics bunch of girls and their families uses Chantilly perfume."

"Chantilly? Um, you gotta start with Larisa's mother, then Larisa, then Erin, then Linda and then the rest of the girls."

"Linda uses it?"

"Occasionally, why?"

"I'll tell you later. Does Linda buy it?"

"I don't know. You asked me who uses it, I told you who I've noticed, starting with the heaviest user on down."

"Mrs. Cumiskey uses a lot?"

"Well, I shouldn't have said heaviest user. It's just that real perfume causes different reactions on different people. The same amount I use might smell like twice as much on her. Let's just say it's her trademark. Larisa got the rest of the girls using it. You know I'm not gonna leave you alone until you tell me why you're asking."

"Trust me, please. I will tell you, but later."

I was preoccupied at lunch, dying to think of a way to broach the subject I had been thinking about constantly, even during the murder investigation. Margo was cheery and fun to talk to, but everything was peripheral. She wasn't playing dumb or hard to get. I knew she knew I was interested in her again, but she didn't know how to react either. She had to protect herself from getting hurt again. I had to show her that because of the changes in both of us—not just in her (which were more obvious)—we would not run into the same kinds of problems again, that she would not need time to sort it all out, but that if she did, I would be willing to allow that without dumping on her.

"I thought we'd come here to symbolize an attempt at a new start," I tried.

"That was a good idea, Philip," she said, earnestly. "I would have felt uncomfortable at one of our old haunts."

"But you feel more comfortable here?"

"A little."

"You're not comfortable with me?"

"Not totally. We've been through a lot, Philip, and I don't know what I feel for you. I feel it very deeply, whatever it is, but even with all the time I've had, I don't know if it's just gratitude, appreciation, friendliness, or what."

"I know what I feel for you, Margo."

"Do you? Really? Or are you just guessing too?"

"I know for sure, but I'm hesitant to burden you with it just now when you're doing so well."

"Your feelings for me will be a burden?"

"Sometimes I think so. They were in the past."

"It wasn't your feelings then; it was your reaction to my feelings."

"What I'm getting at, Margo, is that I am surer about how I feel about you now than I've ever been, but if you're not ready, I don't want to push you. You're blossoming into such beauty, inner beauty to match your looks. Looks. What a weak word. You know what I think is physically beautiful about you?"

"Are you going to embarrass me, Philip?"

"I imagine. But let me tell you anyway. It's how you move, your hands, your fingers. Your face and hair, of course. That's obvious to everyone. But I appreciate the whole picture."

She studied her menu, and I hoped I hadn't sounded corny.

We ordered and were both grateful, I think, for the lull in the conversation. But as we waited to be served, I wanted to make her feel more at ease. "If you're not ready for me, I understand. I really don't have any more patience than I used to, but you are worth the wait. I can hardly believe I almost lost you for good."

"If I wasn't ready for you, would I have come to lunch with you?"

"I don't know, would you have?"

"No, I would not."

Chapter Nine

By Monday morning, Earl wanted Bonnie and Erin checked out of their hotel room and moved back into Bonnie's place. He asked her if she was ready to come back to work, knowing full well that Sgt. Festschrift, at least, would want to question her.

Larry Shipman came in early, none the worse for wear after his brief stay in the cooler at the 19th precinct.

And while we hadn't even told each other yet, Margo and I were in love again. She wasn't ready to make any commitments about the future, but I felt she was mine, and I *knew* I was hers.

Erin, who would be bored staying at her grandmother's place, asked if she could go to Cumiskeys' and stay with Larisa. Earl said he thought it would be all right if it was OK with the Cumiskeys and Bonnie. It was.

But when the morning paper was delivered and the murder weapon was described, things began to happen. Included in the story was the news that although Linda Gibbons's fingerprints were found on the car, so were two other sets of prints, as yet unidentified. The police were seeking to fingerprint anyone associated with the case, and many were balking at the prospect. But one was not.

Greg Gibbons not only came forward, willing to be

fingerprinted, but he also told police that they would likely find his prints on the car. "There is a reason they're there, but that will be your problem to figure out." He was printed, the prints were matched, and he was booked, demanding that his wife be freed. She was not.

Festschrift would not comment for the press; he told Earl, however, that he couldn't decide which suspect had the best motive. "I know he was in the vicinity of that parking lot that night though, don't I?"

"Do you?" Earl asked.

"He met with Mr. Cumiskey at the donut shop later."

"So why don't you bust Mr. Cumiskey then? And Coach Adamski, Bonnie, Erin, everybody?"

"If I find their prints on that car, you can bet I will, Earl. You can bet I will."

About midday, Earl took another call from Festschrift, who wanted to question Erin. Earl told him she was not home or at Bonnie's and that he preferred not to tell him where she was.

"Her parents are both in jail, and the man who split them up has been murdered, Earl," Festschrift said. "You think I can traumatize her any more?"

"She'll be at the Cumiskey home," Earl finally conceded. "I'll call out there and tell them you should be allowed to talk with her privately this evening."

"I'd appreciate that very much, Earl," Festschrift said, as if maybe he really didn't and expected nothing less.

"Would you mind, however, if I sent someone out there to be with her?"

"Like a lawyer maybe?"

"Maybe. No, seriously, Wally, we're talking about a child away from home here. Let me have Margo and Philip go out there with you. In fact, come by here and they'll drive out with you."

"Fair enough. Will you be there?"

"Probably not; I've got my own leads to follow up."

"You sharing all your leads with me?"

"Ask yourself the same question, Wally. 'Bye now."

Earl and Larry spent the afternoon at Linda's apartment with a key provided by Bonnie. They had convinced her that Linda's and Erin's best interests were at heart and that they should search the place thoroughly before the police did so there would be no surprises. "The only rub, Bon," Earl said, "is that if I find anything incriminating, I'm going to have to share it with Sergeant Festschrift." She nodded and gave him the keys.

Earl and Larry called from Linda's apartment a couple of hours later. "Would Erin have taken her mother's overnight bag and left her own?" they asked Bonnie.

"Oh sure, she does that frequently. Switches off."

"Does Linda ever use Erin's overnight bag?"

"I don't think so, no."

"Put Philip on the phone, please."

"Yes, Earl, Philip here."

"Philip, I want you to call Festschrift and ask him to meet me at Linda Gibbons's apartment. And I want you to beat him here, hear?"

"Yeah."

I raced over to Linda's, but I arrived only a few minutes before Festschrift and one of his men. "Can't you see the

111

signs on the door, Earl!" Wally demanded. "It says it's off limits until we've been through it."

"So what're you going to do, book me for violating a police barrier? You know I wouldn't keep anything important from you. Besides, you don't need to go through it any more, Wally," Earl said. "Larry here found what we've all been looking for. He grasped it with a tweezers and plastic bagged it for you, so all you have to do is match it, fingerprint it, and pick up another suspect."

Larry produced a Baggie containing the broken off handle of a lady's purple razor.

"Where'd you find it?" Festschrift asked.

"In this overnight bag. Erin's name is on it."

"How come she didn't take it with her to her girlfriend's house?" Wally's partner asked.

"Who knows?" Shipman said. "Maybe she took her mother's just to feel closer to her right now."

"What do you make of this, Earl?" Wally asked. "I don't mind tellin' ya, I'm stumped. What have we got here, a family murder?"

"Unlikely. But they *were* all there. Each had a motive. Two have fingerprints on the car, and the daughter has the hand strength to do it. I hate to say it, but I have to concede that among the three of them, you probably have your man."

"Or woman," Festschrift said. "Or child. You wanna come with me when I pick her up?"

"This is a very unusual situation, honey," Festschrift told Erin an hour later in the car. "We have a warrant for

112

your arrest, but because you are a minor, we must secure a lawyer for you before we ask you anything. Mr. Haymeyer here will serve as your guardian while you're downtown, in the, uh, absence of your parents."

"I don't care if I have a lawyer or not, Mr. Haymeyer," Erin said. "I won't be answering any questions or offering any information."

She sounded so grownup it was disarming. But for the rest of the trip downtown, she said nothing. At the precinct station, she was assigned a lawyer and a custodian, and Festschrift and Earl and I headed back out to the Cumiskeys'. Larisa was still at school when Ernest and Jean sent the twins out to play and took us into their fashionable family room.

Ernest sat with his arm around his wife, seeming very subdued compared to the shows I had seen him put on at gymnastics meets. Before the competition he would greet all his friends and other fathers of gymnasts with very physical handshakes, hugs, pats on the head, the whole bit. A real outgoing, boisterous type. Then, during the meet, depending upon how Larisa was doing, he could be seen going through any number of gyrations, shouting, turning red, fuming, pacing, stomping. If she lost, he'd storm off to the car. If she won, he was more gregarious than ever, again greeting everyone with a cupped-hand smack on the cheek or a slap on the shoulder. When he wanted to, he could make you feel like a million bucks.

This evening, he was merely subdued. "You wanna do the talking, honey?" he said.

His wife, smelling heavily of Chantilly, leaned forward

on the edge of a couch facing us. Her husband's hand still rested on her back.

"Yes, well, gentlemen, this is not an easy thing to say. We love Erin like our own daughter. They get along so well together and enjoy each other so. You know, even with the difference in ages, there is no problem. However, you might think that Larisa, being older, would be a good influence on young Erin and make her want to act older. In many ways, this is true and it works out that way."

Mrs. Cumiskey was a handsome, deeply tanned woman with short hair and stylish sports clothes. She appeared to be the country club type that she was.

"However, in some other ways, I have to admit that Erin has also been an influence upon Larisa. Sometimes when several of the girls are over for a slumber party, which we let Larisa have at least once a month, usually more often because we are more fortunate than some"— and here both made unsuccessful attempts to appear humbly grateful for their opulence—"well, occasionally the girls get tired and silly and giddy."

"Yes," Festschrift said, pushing her, "and they do things they might not otherwise do? Things that girls only Erin's age might do, even though she's the only one under sixteen in the bunch?"

"Yes, that's right," she said, almost smiling. "But frankly, we've run into things that are embarassing. Things we wish they hadn't done, regardless how playful or seemingly innocent."

"And you've discovered something more?" Festschrift tried again. "Something that concerns you, especially in light of what's happened."

"Yes," she said, "especially in light of what's happened."

"That's right," Ernest said, as only he could, as if he had so liked the way Festschrift and his wife had put it, "very much so in light of what's happened." He ran his palm up to the back of his wife's head and let it linger in her hair.

She stood and hurried quietly to a desk in the corner and dug a sheaf of papers from a bottom drawer. "My husband was not very pleased to find these, I must say," she said, returning and sitting closer to him. He leaned forward with his arm around her back to look at them with her. We all edged forward too, but she wasn't quite ready to let us study them.

"You should say I was disappointed," he said. "Very, very disappointed. I didn't find them funny at all."

"No, he, well, neither of us found them funny in the least. He was very disappointed. And I would say upset."

"Yes, I *was* upset, that's right. Upset."

The stack consisted of white notebook paper with blue lines and three holes in one side. The writing, from my perspective, was girlish with back-slanted and heavily rounded letters with stars or flowers rather than dots over each *i*, and lots of underlining.

"I might as well tell you from the outset that these *are* in my daughter's handwriting," Mrs. Cumiskey said.

"Yes," her husband agreed. "There'll be no hiding

that. You could have found that out very easily, and I should say that we could have burned these papers very easily as well. However, we didn't and I felt, we felt, that you should see them and be aware of them. Go ahead, honey."

Festschrift shifted impatiently. "Why not give them to us one at a time, starting with me," he suggested, "and we'll read them in sequence. That way you won't have to read them aloud."

The officious husband took them from her and began peeling them off one by one to Wally, who read each stonily and passed them on to Earl and then to me. Wally shook his head occasionally, and Earl grunted now and then. Finally, the first of several sheets came to me. It may have been in Larisa's handwriting, but it was likely dictated by several girls in the wee hours of some slumber party morning when they were in some kind of a mood. Here's what Larisa wrote:

My name is Erin Gibbons and I'm thirteen years old. My friend Larisa Cumiskey and I will one day rule the gymnastics world as the best in every event. We don't care who's first or who's second, as long as each is one of us.

My mother has forced my father to leave us because she is seeing another man, a man named John Bizell. He drives a silver Corvette, and some might say he is good looking, but he is not a good man.

I have been watching them for some time now, and my friends and I, all the girls on Nik Adamski's AAU Gymnastics team, are getting ready to ambush him. That's right, literally ambush him.

We know where he works, because he works where my dad works. And we know his hours, because we know when he most often comes to see my mother. Since my father moved out, he doesn't even try to be gone by the time I get home.

We will ask Larisa's father to get us some guns because he can get a good price on anything. Maybe we'll rent them, because we won't have any more need for them after we shoot Mr. Bizell and any police who try to get in our way. The only person we will try to protect will be my father and my mother if she says she is sorry it happened.

We'll wait for him to arrive at our apartment, then I'll make an excuse to go out. I'll call all my team-mates, and they will meet me at the corner. Larisa will bring the guns in a grocery bag. We'll hide behind the other parked cars and when he comes out to get in his car, we'll all shoot at him from different directions to make sure somebody gets him.

We'll make sure he's dead by cutting his heart out. Larisa's father can also get a good price on a big knife.

Then, with nothing for me to worry about any-more, nothing to bother me when I practice, Larisa and I will just have to keep getting better so we can be the best in the world, the best ever. And Mr. Cumiskey will be glad he provided the guns and the knife, but he will never know the reason.

"Did the girls ever mention anything like this to either of you?" Festschrift asked. Mrs. Cumiskey shook her head. Her husband spoke.

"Of course not. It's just a little girl's fantasy and I'm embarrassed that my daughter let herself be dragged into it. She hates violence and would be scared to death of a gun or a knife."

"If you're convinced it's just a little girl's fantasy, Mr. Cumiskey, why did you feel it necessary to show it to us?"

"Because the little girl's fantasy came true, didn't it? I just thought you should be aware of it. Plus, if any of the other girls who were here that night feel guilty about it, they might mention it and it could look bad for both Erin and Larisa."

"And you want it to look bad only for Erin, is that it?"

"Why, no! But, but—well, Larisa had no reason, I mean. Oh, come now, you're not seriously suggesting that Larisa—"

"No," Festschrift said. "I just want to know what you think about Erin. Could she have murdered this man?"

"I don't think so," Mrs. Cumiskey said.

"I wouldn't be too sure," Ernest said. "I've heard her talk about him. She hated him. She blamed him for everything. She even blamed the fact that she was troubled about him for her scores being lower than she thought they could have been, and at that time she was number one in two events. I think she's capable of getting rid of or stepping over anything that gets in the way of her winning."

Mrs. Cumiskey appeared a bit startled by such a harsh statement and flashed a doubtful look at her husband.

"Oh, Ern, I think she's a little too sweet for all that, isn't she?"

And he finally got excited. "Are you kidding me? Have you seen that look of hers when she walks up to the beam or onto the mat? I'm telling you, the girl has a winning determination about her. She ought to, she learned it from the best. You fellas wanna see the gallery of fame I've built for Larisa?"

"Ernie, please, I don't think that would be appropriate under the circumstances—"

"Nonsense! You guys would have time for a little peek, wouldn't ya? It'll only take a second."

There was nothing we could say. "I've not got a lot of time," Festschrift growled, "but sure, let's have a look."

Mrs. Cumiskey excused herself, and we were ushered upstairs to Ernest's paneled den, which was as large as most people's rec rooms. On the walls he had awards from every company he had ever worked for, plus a couple of certificates naming him first in his class at some sales or management course.

"Got all your awards here, huh?" Earl said cordially.

"Nope. Just the first places, the number ones. I've got a raft of seconds in my time, but I don't keep those. Anything less than first is last, I always say. The philosophy hasn't hurt my career, I'll tell you that."

A couple of dozen pictures of Larisa, all of her waving from the top step of the awards platform, graced the walls. "I used to put up a picture every time she won an event," he said, "but now, at her level of skill and accomplishment, the only things that count are winning the all-around competition. I've got this nice big one here of her first perfect ten score, but I'm leaving room for the world's championship in Helsinki next month and of course the Olympics. That will be the ultimate. Her first Olympic gold. I can hardly wait."

"I'll bet you'd put up a picture of her from the Olympics, win, lose, or draw," Earl said. "Am I right?"

Cumiskey appeared annoyed by the question, but he broke into a grin and threw his arm around Haymeyer's neck, forcing Earl's head into the crook of his elbow and pretending to batter him with his other hand. "Don't even mention such a thing, you sonofagun!" he said, laughing. Earl tried to smile.

And we left.

Chapter Ten

"I'm gonna do somethin' crazy," Festschrift said in the car. "I've had it with this case!"

"This is a little early for you to be giving it up, isn't it, Wal'?" Haymeyer said. "We've only been on the chase less than forty-eight hours."

"Yeah, but I've got too many suspects, and I don't like any one of 'em. If this was a crime of passion, any one of 'em coulda done it, but none rings true with me."

"Me either," Earl conceded. "But we're gonna have a tough time getting around that razor handle."

"Yeah, especially if it's got Erin's fingerprints on it. Let's call and find out, because if it doesn't, I'm gonna see if I can't get all three of 'em released."

I couldn't believe my ears. Neither, apparently, could Earl.

"You've got to be kidding," he said.

"No, I'm not. Even if one of them is the murderer, letting them off on their own recognizance won't threaten the case. It's not like they're gonna try to kill anybody else except those of us trying to find the truth, and we're not worried about that, are we?"

Earl shook his head, still wondering what Festschrift was up to and whether he'd really go ahead with this weird scheme. Yet when I thought about it, I wasn't worried about either Linda or Erin actually harming me. Greg I hardly knew.

"If I let 'em out, I think each of us should take one of 'em, and I'd like the little girl."

"What do you mean, 'take' one of them?" Earl said.

"Question them, stay with them, try to learn where they're coming from. See if we can trip them up. You know what else I'm concerned about, and what your Margo can help with?"

"What's that?"

"I'm a little uncomfortable with Mrs. Murray's actions Saturday morning. Could she have planted that razor handle and then hit the road?"

Earl scratched his head. "Where *do* you come up with these, Wally? What would she be up to?"

"I'm talkin' about whether she could have done it."

"Nah, I'm not accepting that yet."

"But you're open to it?"

"No, not really, no."

"Earl," I asked, "what would you and Sergeant Festschrift think of my going back to the Cumiskey's tonight, sort of unannounced, to ask if I can chat with Larisa as a friend?"

"*Are* you a friend?" Festschrift asked.

"Yes, he is," Earl said. "He's been following Erin and Larisa for some time. It might not be a bad idea."

"It's awright with me," Wally said, "'cause it'll take me time to get these three released anyway. I'm gonna have to talk to each of 'em first. Ooh, the press is not

122

gonna believe this! They'll put their front pages together with the news that an entire family is in custody for murder, and by the time the papers hit the street, they'll be wrong!"

"You're really gonna go through with this?"

"I am. Maybe I'm ready for the nut house, but let's you and me and Philip and my partner and the crime lab keep that razor to ourselves and see who's the first suspect—or nonsuspect—to say something about it, something they shouldn't know."

"That sounds like a lot of people to keep a secret," I said.

"It is. But are you gonna be the one who blows it?"

"No."

"Is Earl?"

"No," I said again.

"Well, I know my partner, who is off the next three days, and he never breaks a confidence. And do you know that the crime lab people can't talk outside the room or they automatically lose their jobs?"

"Is that right? Well, maybe you *can* pull it off."

Wally and Earl dropped me off at the office, where I learned that Bonnie would be spending the night with Margo. Shipman was busy with Earl's other cases, trying to keep the business going while the rest of us found ourselves up to our necks in the Bizell case. Margo was becoming antsy and wanted to get in on the action.

"I'll be all right at your place if I know you'll be back later," Bonnie said. "You go with Philip."

"But is that all right with Earl and Sergeant Fest-schrift?" Margo wanted to know.

I was wondering the same thing, but I wanted so badly to talk with Margo alone and to have her along that I assured her it was fine. "I'll take the heat for it if it's not," I said.

"I'm not concerned with who takes the heat, Philip," Margo said. "I just don't want to go if it wouldn't be right."

"It's all right," I said. "Come on."

We were only a few miles up the Edens when Margo admitted, "I'm glad I came."

"I am too."

"I love Bonnie, but I get tired of her crying and moaning all day long. I don't know what else to say or do for her. You know she's convinced that either Linda or Erin killed Bizell, and I think she's leaning toward Linda."

"Is that right? I think Greg thinks it was Linda too; that's why he's turned himself in. There's probably a logical reason for his fingerprints on Bizell's car. They work out of the same office, don't they? They probably park in the same lot. He could have leaned on the door while chatting with Bizell or something."

"But would they chat? It seems like they'd be having a cold war these days, wouldn't they, Philip?"

"Maybe, but remember, Johnny hasn't seen Linda for a month."

"So Linda says, but we know her prints were on the car

too, so she must have seen him not long before he died. Are you ruling out Greg as a suspect, Philip?"

"I think so. If it was Greg, how could he have planted the other part of the razor in Linda's apartment?"

"Planted what?"

I winced. "Oh, no! I promised Festschrift and Earl I would say nothing to anyone! I can't believe I did that! Margo, you hafta promise not to repeat that, especially to Bonnie, no, not to anyone. They're trying to flush out the murderer with information only he or she would know about."

"Well, I'm not the murderer, Philip, and I'll promise to keep it quiet if you tell me what you're talking about. You found the other half of the razor at Linda's?"

"Shipman did. It was in a soft, zipper-style overnight kit of Erin's."

Margo was silent, thinking.

"You think that incriminates anyone other than Erin?" I asked.

"Well, Philip, we can't be naive about Greg's access to the apartment. He must have a key."

"I never thought of that. I also forgot that the one name Festschrift didn't mention when he rattled off the list of people who had to keep our discovery a secret was that of the guy who found it."

"Larry? He'd never leak a secret."

"I know. But he doesn't know it's a secret. I'd better try to reach him."

I pulled off to a gas station and found a pay phone. I

couldn't reach him at the office or at home, and I couldn't exactly call Bonnie at Margo's place and leave a message. Margo and I didn't know what else to do except pray that he would somehow not talk about it to anyone.

"I missed you today, Margo," I said.

"I missed you too, and I'm not just saying that, Philip. I know it's the natural response, but that hasn't been a natural feeling for me until today."

"Ouch. You mean you haven't missed me for so long you were getting used to being without me?"

"Oh, you know I missed you when we first broke up. That was a miserable time. But it did start to get better, the more I got active and the more I relied on God. That's one thing I must not do this time, Philip. I must not switch my reliance from God to you."

"You can count on me for some things, can't you? I need to feel needed."

"Of course. I learned that when I started missing you today. I think I missed hearing that someone loves everything about me, not just my face or even just my character, but even the way I move—was that what you said yesterday?"

"Yeah," I said, embarrassed. "You didn't think it was corny, then?"

"Of course I did, but I love corn. I eat it up."

We both laughed. "You eat it with butter and salt, don't you?" I said.

"Canned, popped, or on the cob," she said and leaned close. "You can be as corny as you want with me, Philip Spence."

"You're a crazy girl," I said.

"And you love it."

"You."

"Hm?"

"I love *you*."

"Thank you," she said, not flippantly. "It's good to have you knowing that I love you again."

"You love me again?" I asked.

"No, I never quit. It's just good to have you aware of it again."

"You're right that I wasn't aware of it. You hid it well."

"I thought I should. I didn't know if it would be returned or not."

"I probably never quit loving you either, Margo, but I didn't know it."

"I know."

"You do?"

"I think I do. I could see it when you got back from Israel. I didn't know if it was pity or remorse or love, but then I never knew that for sure about your love for me from the beginning."

"Do you now?"

"I'm just gonna take your word for it."

"You do that."

"Is Larisa home?" I asked Mrs. Cumiskey at the front door.

"Well, yes, as a matter of fact she came home early from practice, and I don't believe she's feeling well." She lowered her voice. "Her father is not real excited about

127

her missing practice so close to the big meets, especially when she's undisputed leader right now. Ernest and she are not speaking right now, if you know what I mean."

"Well, is she ill?" Margo asked. "Because if she is, we could come back another time. We just thought we'd see how she was doing during this difficult time for everybody."

"Let me see if she feels up to talking. Come in."

Mrs. Cumiskey trotted upstairs and we could hear her husband railing before she shushed him. ". . . chance to be the best in the world and she spends her evenings moping around the —"

Apparently Larisa thought we were worth seeing. She bounded past her mother and down the stairs and right into Margo's arms. "Margo, Philip, thanks for coming. Come on into the family room." She had been crying.

We sat on either side of her on a huge couch. Her brothers were outside shooting a basketball. We hadn't even said anything when she hid her face in her hands and began crying again. She leaned over onto Margo who stroked her hair. "It's all right, 'Risa," Margo said quietly. "It's all right; we're with you and we love you."

She sat up and tried to stop crying. "It's all my fault!" she said. "If I had just thrown away those silly papers. All we were doing was humoring Erin. We never intended to do anything to that Bizell guy. You saw the papers, Philip, do you think they looked serious? We were just being crazy, writing out a fantasy. It made Erin feel better and that's all we cared about."

If this was an act, she was one great actress. "It's not

like I left them out for Daddy to find. He had to ransack my room to come up with them. They weren't just tucked in a drawer somewhere, Margo, they were at the bottom, *beneath* the bottom. My mother lines my drawers with paper, and this stuff was *under* that paper!"

"Why would he do that?" Margo asked.

"I don't know. Doesn't trust me, I guess. More likely, he's just looking for an edge for me over Erin. Well, I've got it now and I can't concentrate enough to take advantage of it. I hope he's satisfied."

"Why did you keep those papers, Larisa?" I asked.

"That's just it. If they had been serious, we'd have gotten rid of them, burned them! That's what Daddy should have done, especially after getting my side of the story. But we added to them each time the girls got together. That wasn't written all at one time. It was just silliness. I'll tell you, it sure freaked out the other girls when we heard about the murder, though. Not that any of us suspected Erin or anything. It was just eerie. I wonder what Daddy thought then."

I looked at Margo. "You mean he found those papers before Bizell was murdered?"

"Oh, yes, probably a month ago. That's why I think he just wanted to use them to scare Erin. She knew, just like all the other girls, that he had found them, and they were all scared their parents would find out. Not as scared as they were when they heard the news, though."

"I imagine not," I said.

"Larisa, what's the matter today? Is it just too much for you to think about Erin under suspicion?"

The high schooler nodded, fighting tears again. "I can't believe Erin had anything to do with it at all!"

"Well, if she didn't, she'll be cleared. You know that, don't you?"

"I guess. But that razor business makes me wonder, and I feel horribly guilty for even letting it enter my mind."

I stiffened. How could she know about the razor? Or was she even thinking of the same thing I was?

"What razor?" Margo asked.

"The newspaper said they had determined that the murder weapon was a lady's razor with half the blade exposed. Oh, Margo, I don't know what to think!" And we were back to tears and tissues and stroking her hair again.

My heart was pounding. Why was this girl associating the murder weapon so strongly with Erin if she didn't know the other half of it had been found in Erin's bag?

"You think because Erin uses that kind of a razor that she could have used one on Johnny Bizell?" Margo asked as gently as she could.

"I don't wanna think that, especially since she got started on that kind of razor at another slumber party here."

"Honey, lots of girls use that brand. It's very popular."

"I know." She didn't want to talk anymore. I gave Margo the eye that we had to get to the bottom of this. "I don't believe Erin murdered Johnny," Larisa said slowly. "I just want the doubts out of my head so I can concentrate on my gymnastics. So I can concentrate on *anything*."

Margo was silent. I took up the conversation. "Why do you have doubts?"

"I don't wanna talk about it anymore."

"I don't blame you, Larisa," I said. "But maybe I can allay your suspicions. Isn't it significant that hundreds of thousands of razors just like that one that killed Johnny Bizell are sold in the Chicago area every year?"

She nodded, but I could tell she was unconvinced. For some reason, she was putting that razor together with Erin when there was no solid connection she should know about.

"Thanks for coming," she said, standing. "You really did help a lot, and I appreciate it."

"You want some good news?" I asked, trying a different tack.

"Sure."

"I think the whole Gibbons family will be released before tomorrow."

"You're serious? Oh, that's great! How did they get around Erin's broken razor? Or didn't she even tell them? I guess she wouldn't have had to tell them, would she? Unless they asked."

I was stunned. "What are you talking about, Larisa?"

"You mean *you* don't know about it?"

"I didn't say that. I want to know what *you* know about it."

"Oh, Philip, I can't say anything about it if *she* didn't,

but I hope she's being cleared in spite of it because it was the only reason I couldn't shake my doubts."

Margo said, "Larisa, do you trust us?" She nodded, but I tried to signal Margo not to say any more. As it turned out, she wasn't giving anything away anyway. "I need you to tell me what you know about Erin's broken razor. It's very important."

Margo said it with such sincerity and urgency that Larisa sat back down, cleared her face vigorously with a tissue, and told us an ominous story.

"I broke that razor myself," she said. "We were going to have a slumber party, and I had agreed to pick up Erin after school and drive her first to practice and then to my house. I drove over to the junior high and parked in a no parking zone. I ran in, laughing and yelling at her to hurry up because I was going to get a ticket. So, she hauled everything out of her locker and started throwing it at me. I caught most of it, but I was falling backward when she tossed her little overnight kit and it slid under my foot. I skipped to keep my balance and stepped right on it and heard something snap. We peeked in the bag in the car to see what I broke and I saw that razor, split right at the top, exposing the blade. I told her to be careful when she threw it away, and we remarked how lucky I had been that it hadn't sliced through the bag and my foot. I remember Erin said something like, 'Yeah, it could've cost you your ranking as the number two girl on our team.' We always kid each other like that.

"Anyway, that's the last I saw that broken razor and the last I thought about it until I read the paper this morning.

Whatever you do, don't breathe a word of this to my dad. He'll have her strung up without thinking twice. But I don't care what that broken razor means, I won't believe Erin murdered anyone unless she tells me herself."

Chapter Eleven

Margo and I stopped to grab a sandwich on the way back to Glencoe, then I dropped her off at her car near the office and ran up to talk to Earl in his apartment, just down from mine.

"How'd it go downtown?" I asked.

"Everything's still up in the air, Philip," he said. "If this weren't so serious it would have made for a great comedy today. Every time Wally tried to release one of the Gibbonses, the suspect would confess to the murder and try to tell how he or she did it. Each thought one of the other two was guilty and tried to take the credit. What makes it more confusing is that now Wally is convinced that *none* of them had anything to do with it."

"Why? And isn't it going to be difficult to release them when they have made confessions?"

"That's just it; their confessions gave them away. All three of them described killing Bizell by surprising him, coming through the passenger door and slashing away at him. But the only wound other than to his neck was that minor gash on his left hand from trying to open his own door. Wouldn't you think he would have fended off the attacker with his hands if he had been approached from the other side?"

"Yeah, but that doesn't prove one of them wasn't telling the truth."

"There's more, Philip. Festschrift told me tonight that before we got to the scene and Shipman badgered him to open the passenger door, he had already had to nearly lie across the victim to reach the door lock with his wire. Then he could open the door when Shipman asked, but it had been locked."

"Yeah?"

"Yes, and how many murderers do you know who surprise a driver by coming through the passenger door, sinking a razor deep into his neck—which the coroner insists could not have been done without considerable pressure and not by a swiping motion—and then backing out and locking the door before shutting it? It's absurd."

"But not impossible."

"Granted, but here's the kicker. Wally gave them each one last chance to prove their claims. He asked them where they got the murder weapon, where the other piece of it was, whether their fingerprints should still be on it, and where was the location of Bizell's car at the time of the murder."

"How'd they do on those?"

"Laughable again. Greg said he bought the razor and hoped to make the murder look as if it were committed by a woman, but not by his wife because he didn't think she used that brand razor. He also said he broke the razor on Bizell's neck and threw the handle away as he ran and that we'd probably find it in the parking lot of the school with his fingerprints on it."

"You're sure this is all full of holes?"

"As sure as I'm sittin' here. You wanna know where he said the murder occurred? In the northeast corner of the parking lot."

"Not even close," I admitted. "Could he have been mixed up in his directions?"

"Nah, Philip. Think. Even if he had the wrong corner, all the corners are exposed. There's no way to commit a murder in any corner of that lot and have it go undiscovered for hours. Impossible."

"Is there any chance he could have changed his mind about protecting his wife and daughter and misled Festschrift on purpose?"

"No."

"So what was Linda's story?"

"She said the razor was one of her own, that she broke it and threw the other part away and stashed the blade end in her purse until the time was right. I loved that. She wants us to believe that she carried that thing around until she happened to run into Bizell at a gymnastics meet. She said the broken part would have been tossed with the garbage weeks ago, and she placed Bizell's car with all the other cars in the lot, not secluded between the garbage bins and the air-conditioning units. Festschrift asked her if she hadn't read in the paper about how the car wasn't discovered until some time after all the other cars were gone. If she had murdered him between the end of the meet and when she met her daughter at the car, surely someone would have seen the car sooner. She said it was parked at one end away from the parking lot lights."

I was tired. I stretched out on Earl's floor and asked about Erin's account.

He said Festschrift was pleasantly surprised to get anything out of her and assumed that when he said he was letting her go, she figured her mother had been exposed. "So, she concocted her own story, which Festschrift could have believed except that he had already learned that the razor handle had no prints on it."

"*No* prints?"

"None."

"What do you make of that, Earl?"

"What do you make of it, junior deputy?"

"That it was a plant. If Erin had just left it in her overnight kit, it would have her prints on it. It was wiped clean?"

"Clean. Very good, Philip. You're gonna make it after all. But there's another reason we know it wasn't Erin. She could have told us that we'd find the razor handle in her overnight bag in the apartment."

"And she didn't?"

"How could she? She didn't know it was there."

"How can you be sure, Earl?"

"Because she *wanted* credit for this murder. That's the best way she could have gotten it, to point us right to the other piece of the murder weapon. But she couldn't do it. She was closer than anyone to guessing the location of Bizell's car, but that's all it was, a guess. She says she sat in the car with Bizell and talked to him, then surprised him with the blade. Wally was beautiful on this one. He

138

asked if she was right-handed. She said of course. He said she was lying. The only way to inflict that wound on Bizell by sitting next to him would be by a left-hander getting his elbow up and back behind the headrest, then plunging the blade in. Wally can visualize the murder now. It was someone reaching in from the driver's side window and getting his hand around behind Johnny's neck and up near the front on the right side."

"Then he couldn't have seen it coming."

"Or if he did, he didn't see it as menacing. That makes me wonder if it was a woman leaning in and embracing him or taking his head in her hand."

"But if not Linda or Erin, who, Earl?"

The phone rang. It was Margo. She told Earl that Bonnie was no longer at her place, nor at her own. "Don't worry yet, Mar," Earl said. "We'll find her."

"Bonnie?" I asked.

"Yeah, shoot. This is all we need. Let's check the office." As we hurried down the hall, Earl assured me that he didn't think Bonnie could have murdered Bizell. "He wouldn't exactly let her get her arms around him while he sits in his car either, you think?"

I had to chuckle at the thought.

"Hey, here's a note from Larry." Earl tried to decipher it as Margo entered.

"What do you think?" she said. "Where could she be?"

"She's with Larry," Earl said. "Did you try to call there?"

"No, I didn't think of it," she said, dialing.

Earl motioned me over. I looked at the note over his shoulder. It read:

See you soon.

Under the circumstances,

I thought it would be all right to

counsel Mrs. Murray over dinner.

I will call before bringing her back.

Don't worry about her.

All is fine. Be back soon.

Larry

"There's no answer, Earl, but I guess we needn't worry if Larry is with her. Earl?"

He was still studying the note. I had read it and turned away. I turned back. "What is it, Earl?"

"Larry's handwriting. It's never been this neat. And why the big explanation? Why not his usual 'Bonnie and I have gone to dinner'? He's trying to tell us something."

Margo joined us and read it carefully. "It's as plain as day," she said, dread in her voice. "Just read the first letter of each line."

Earl swore. "She thinks her daughter killed Bizell, I'll bet anything," he said. "We need to tell her otherwise. It wasn't Erin either, not even Greg."

"Our possibilities are narrowing," Margo said.

"My money is on the Cumiskey twins," I said, trying to be funny. Neither Margo nor Earl appreciated it.

"All we can do is wait for them," Earl said. "Who knows where he might have taken her? I've never known him to go to the same place twice without being dragged.

140

Anyway, I'm glad you're both here. I wanted to talk to you."

Margo and I looked at each other and followed Earl back to his office. He dragged his chair out from behind the desk and rolled it up next to the two side chairs. He offered his chair to Margo, and we all sat down. "I don't know how to tell you this," he said, "but I have been talking to Wally Festschrift about God."

Nonplussed is too weak a word for our reaction. "I, you, wha—?"

"I know it sounds crazy. And mostly, I've felt inadequate."

"But, but—"

"I know, Philip. I'm not even qualified. It's not like I'm trying to even give him something I've got because as you both well know, and as Festschrift himself would say it, 'I ain't got it myself.' But if there was ever a person who needed and could use what you two have, it's Wally Festschrift."

"And so you're, I mean—"

"Yes. I'm telling him. What do *you* call it? Witnessing?"

You're witnessing to Festschrift?" I finally managed. "But, witnessing is—"

"I know, Philip. It's telling about something you have personal knowledge of. Legally it means giving an eyewitness account."

Earl sat there waiting for further reaction. I had none.

"Are you trying to tell us something, Earl?" Margo tried.

141

"No, as I said, 'I ain't got it myself,' but I'm telling it anyway."

"Uh, just what are you telling him?" I asked.

"All the stuff you've tried to tell me over the years. I'm sure I'm getting some of it wrong, and that's why I want you to help me. He needs it, kids, and if he's not getting it from you, he's gonna hafta get it from me."

"You've been telling him what?" Margo said. "That he needs God, or religion, or what?"

"Oh, give me credit for more than that! If there's one thing I have gotten out of all your preaching around here—of which there hasn't been much lately, by the way—it's that what you've got and what you've talked about is not religion. It's a *Person*. How'm I doin'?"

"Great. What else did you tell him?"

"I told him that you admit you have done wrong, admit it to God, I mean. And you pray that Christ will forgive you and save you and give you peace. How's that?"

We just sat staring. "That's unbelievable," Margo said.

"That's what I've been saying for two years, Margo," Earl said. "But somehow it makes sense to Festschrift. He's a little embarrassed to ask you any more about it, Philip, but he was impressed with you, I'll say that. We got to reminiscing and reconciling and recreating the old days, and he started telling me how remorseful he was about much of his past. Then it sort of popped out."

"It popped out? What popped out?"

"All that stuff you two have been telling me over the years. Wally was lamenting the fact that you can't turn the

142

clock back, that you have to pay the price for your mistakes, that you can't undo wrongs, and all of a sudden I heard myself telling him that, by God, you *can* let someone else pay the price, and I wasn't swearing."

"How'd he react?"

"Well, if you think you guys were stunned by what I just said, that was the *last* thing Wally Festschrift thought he'd ever hear out of me. But he listened. He always did listen to me, even when I was a brash rookie and he was already the weather-beaten veteran. He told me he was sorry for the way he had treated me over the years, that he didn't know why he'd been that way, and that he had a lot of people to apologize to, including his wife and kids. You know what I told him? You're not gonna believe this."

"Try us," Margo said. "I'll believe anything now."

"I told him, 'See, Wally, we've only been talking about it a few minutes, and it's working already!' He thought that was pretty funny at first, but you know he laughed until he cried. That's when I knew I would have to come back to you and tell you that something struck a chord with him that was never struck with me. At least not until he started crying. That hit me, I don't mind telling you.

"But anyway, I knew I needed more ammunition. What do I tell him now?"

"Would you like us to talk to him, Earl?" I said. "Should I tell him how to receive Christ into his life?"

"I don't think so, Philip. I think he'll take it from me but not from you at this point. There's a lot of complexity in that guy. I thought of your saying that all you have to do

143

is to realize that God loves you and wants to forgive you and become part of you, but all I could think of to tell him was that you just do that by praying and meaning it. But I knew that was too simple, so I didn't say it. I'm here for another crash course."

"You've learned well, Earl," Margo said, her voice unsteady. "You tell him that and get him into a good church, and you'll have your first convert."

"That's all there is to it? I should have known. That's what you've been trying to tell me. I haven't always liked the way you went about it, but I never did find any superiority complex in either of you, and I've been watching for it. I *have* been disappointed in some inconsistencies, especially in you, Philip, but I also know that you've told me a million times to not judge God by His children. I think I know what that means now."

"So where are *you* in all this?" Margo asked.

"How do you mean?"

"I mean what is Earl Haymeyer thinking about what he told Sergeant Festschrift?"

"You mean am I ready?"

"Yeah."

"Let me say it this way. I don't need any more encouragement. If both what I told Festschrift and what I almost told him is on track, then I know all I need to know to make my own choice and take my own action, don't I?"

We nodded.

"Then I will or won't on my own—is that fair enough? That's the way I've always been and the way I always will be. Philip, you told me once that God would take me just as I was, right?"

"Right."

"I resented that then. I thought you were saying I was some no account skid row type. I know what you mean now. If I do want God to take me, He's going to have to take my independence and all the rest."

I wanted to assure him that He would, but silence seemed appropriate. Margo couldn't take her eyes off Earl. He grew restless, embarrassed. "So," he said, slapping his knees with both hands and rising, "if I'm on the right track with Wally, I'll keep at it."

We followed him back out to the main office, our eyes meeting in wonder.

"Let's talk a little business," he said. "Tomorrow morning I'm going to want Larry to meet with the Gibbons family. Believe it or not, our work can sometimes be conciliatory, and I think we have a classic case here of people trying to cover for each other. There's a base of love there, and if nothing else comes out of this crazy case, maybe we can see that family reunited. Do we all agree that this would be a valid goal?"

I was thinking that Earl was right: "It" had started working already.

"Now then," he continued, "if we eliminate Greg and Linda and Erin as suspects, who's left?"

"Don't be so quick to eliminate all of them," Margo cautioned. "Two of them are women, and they might be smart enough to have misled you. You can't tell me that

Erin didn't know that razor handle was still in her overnight bag."

Earl glared at me. "I'm sorry, Earl, it just slipped out, and Margo has told no one, I swear."

"You swear! Honestly, Philip. If that had gone any further it could have affected the interrogations Wally conducted today. What if those suspects had known we had already found that razor piece? They all could have been misleading us!"

"Well, Shipman was never reminded not to say anything."

"He wouldn't—he wasn't? You're right, he wasn't!"

Margo heard a car and stepped to the window. "You can have your fears confirmed or denied in a minute, Earl," she said. "It's them."

Chapter Twelve

"No," Larry said. "Of course I knew better than that. Really, Earl, you insult me."

"Just checking, Larry. I'm sorry."

Earl told Bonnie the good news, and she broke down. Margo appeared troubled because she hadn't shaken her fear that Erin knew more than she was saying, but she was also grateful that Bonnie could stop worrying—even if only temporarily—about the guilt of her daughter and granddaughter.

"You know, I was so afraid that Linda or Erin might have had something to do with Bizell's death that I could have killed myself. I couldn't stand the turmoil in my mind. I didn't want to know the truth if that was it."

"Really?" Earl said, playing dumb but nodding to Larry behind her back to indicate that we had gotten his cryptic message.

Earl gave Larry his assignment for the next morning and suggested he call the parties and arrange for them to get together early. "What I'm going to want to do, besides attempting the reconciliation, is to find out how Greg and Linda really explain their fingerprints on Bizell's car, in light of the fact that it's been shown they didn't murder him."

"I'm curious about that, too," Margo said. "Among other things."

I followed Margo and Bonnie to Margo's place so I could say good-night to Margo in the hall while Bonnie went to bed. I told her about my conversation with Linda Gibbons and how I had sensed the comparison between her story and that of the woman taken in adultery whom Jesus had forgiven in the New Testament.

"And when you hear that Earl is doing our job for us, it makes you want to get back in the game, doesn't it?" she asked.

"You got it."

"I'll be praying for you, Philip. When are you going to try to talk to her?"

"I don't know. Sometime this week. I wish I knew Greg better and whether his plans are to take her back or what, because I think this could be good for him, too."

"You gonna wait until after the big meet tomorrow, or will Erin even be competing?"

"There's a gymnastics meet tomorrow?"

"Only the national regional. One of those do-or-die jobs on the way to the national championships. That's all."

"Where's this being held?"

"At the Rosemont Horizon."

"The Horizon? That's huge."

"Well, there'll be teams from all over the Midwest, even down to Texas. The place is sold out, and the meet will be televised nationally."

The next morning Larry met with Greg and Linda

Gibbons and Erin at Linda Gibbons's apartment while I was tracking down AAU gymnastics coach Nik Adamski. Earl had asked that each of us verify at least one remaining principal's movements from the previous Friday night. Believe it or not, Margo had drawn the Cumiskey family, twins included.

I found Nik Adamski at the Y in Mount Prospect. He was a recreational director there, but he was doing nothing but doodling, experimenting with various lineups, some including Larisa, some not, some including Erin, some not, and some including neither.

"I haf no idea whedder dese girls be wit' me tonight or vat," he explained. "Larisa, she has been down since she lost ze all-around to Erin at Hillside. She say she iss upset about Erin, bot everybody know she can no kill a man, so I think Larisa, she just upset wit' herself."

"Uh, Mr. Adamski, it's part of my job to determine your movements after the meet Friday night."

"Oh?" he said. "Vy is dat? I am suspect?"

"Well, everybody is. I even had to account for where I was."

Unexpectedly, Nik Adamski stood. "I grew up in Poland during de Hitler regime," he said, standing rigidly. "I come here to stop accounting for self. I need tell no one vere I go, vat I do, not'ing."

"You can tell *me*, Mr. Adamski. I can't hurt you. I can help you. If the police ask and you don't tell them, you could be in trouble."

"How can I be in trouble when I have done not'ing?"

"You can't, but you don't want the police bothering

you now, especially when you have so much to do before tonight's meet. It might interest you to know, by the way, that Erin has been released. And I can't imagine Larisa's father allowing Larisa not to compete for any reason."

He sat back down. "Erin released? Dat good news. She be out of shape though. Can't count on first places."

"She competed brilliantly just Friday night," I said. "That's just a few days ago."

"She scored four 9.85s, Mr. Spence. Highest all-around I ever coach. You don't do dat again four days later vit' no work. You don't understand mind. It's not just body. It's mind, and her mind been troubled plenty lately and probably still is. She released, but her mama released too?"

"Yes, and her father."

"But do dey know who kill Bizell?"

"No, do you?"

He glared at me. "Of course not. I never saw de man. Just hear about him everyday for months make me vant to kill him if I did. But if dey not know who kill him, how peaceful can Erin be? She need peace to do well."

"That I don't know. That will bother Larisa too, won't it?"

"Only t'ing bother Larisa is Larisa," he said.

"Still, Coach, could you tell me what you did after Friday's meet, after you talked to Mrs. Murray?"

"Mrs. Murray. I no talk to a Mrs. Murray."

My heart nearly stopped. "You didn't talk to Erin's grandmother about personalized coaching for her this summer?"

"Oh, Erin grandmother. Yah, yah, I did."

150

I breathed again.

"Then what did you do?"

"Was interviewed for local television. Den meet wife at back door and drive home."

I knew it would be easy enough to check. And it was. Nik Adamski was clean, which was no surprise to me, though he threw me with that "I no talk" to Bonnie line.

Margo learned that Mr. Cumiskey "kicked a few chairs—I'm like that when I'm frustrated" and left even before the awards ceremony, "not because I was so upset, though I admit I was, but because I had an appointment with Erin's father about a job interview."

Ernest Cumiskey admitted that it was difficult to work up much enthusiasm for the father of the girl who had swept his daughter in four events, but he had done the best he could. Margo asked him, "Isn't it true that normally you go after only the number one top sellers from other companies?"

He had been flustered. "Why of course, that's my trademark."

She just stared at him, leaving unasked the question of why, then, Greg Gibbons when everyone knew that he wasn't even close to the top salesman in his firm.

"Why Gibbons then, you're wondering?" he said, reddening. "I don't know. Always liked the kid, I guess. I'd seen him around socially, ya know, at meets and stuff. Maybe I wanted to do him a favor for the sake of his daughter. She's a good friend of my daughter, ya know."

"Still, if you don't mind my saying so, you're not known for hiring people to do them favors."

He was getting angry. "Yeah, well, listen, uh—"

151

"Margo Franklin."

"Yeah, Miss Franklin, truth is I was only humoring Gibbons. He came to me, see, and I have a few openings. I knew from the onset that I wouldn't be hiring him, but I thought, hey, what the heck, it'll make him feel good to be interviewed by the president of a top firm, right? Maybe make him look good to his wife. Maybe they can get back together and I can have a little to do with that, huh? You follow?"

"Yes. Very generous of you."

"Yeah."

"And very sacrificial."

"How's that?"

"That you'd set up a strictly cosmetic meeting like that for right after a big international meet. You couldn't have known that your daughter was not going to win. In fact, you probably expected her to win plenty."

"You bet. I always do. I have to get *her* thinking the same way. She'll win everything tonight on national TV. You gonna be there?"

"Wouldn't miss it. But if you don't mind my pressing this point, why would you set up this meaningless meeting that would force you to leave a gymnastics meet so quickly?"

Margo told Earl and me that it was apparent Cumiskey *did* mind her pressing the point, and he told her so. "What are you trying to say, sweetie? I mean I don't mind answerin' a few questions, and you can check with the clerk at the all-night donut shop in the mall over there to see when I met Gibbons and when I left. Now if there's nothing more—"

"No, nothing more." And here Margo tried to change his mood. "You're real optimistic about Larisa's chances tonight?"

"Oh, yeah. There'll be more competition, just in numbers, than there was with the Europeans Friday night, and there are some super American girls too. That gal from Dubuque will be back. But I think without Erin in the lineup, Larisa will rise to the occasion. Could win everything. No flukes tonight."

"Erin's performance Friday was a fluke?"

"Oh, I wouldn't say that, but four 9.85s? Come on. Luck? Coincidence? Not even Larisa has had an all-around score of 39.4. Had 39.3 once. Erin's good. Ought to be; Larisa made her what she is. But they're not really in the same league. Not really. See you tonight?"

After her visit to Cumiskey's office, Margo visited once more with Mrs. Cumiskey.

"We had a report from Mrs. Murray, Erin's grand-mother, that she saw Larisa waiting for you after the meet. We'll have to check on what Larisa did and where she was after that, but would you mind telling me where you were?"

"Not at all," she told Margo patiently. "I don't know if you're aware that my twins are hyperactive?"

Margo shook her head.

"Well, let me tell you, that's bad enough when they're toddlers and preschoolers, but when they hit eight and

153

nine and get some size and can fight each other and everyone else, it's all I can do to keep them reined in."

"I can imagine. So, you were with the boys?"

"Well, yes. I watched the awards ceremony because I wanted to see how Larisa took her disappointment. I thought she did remarkably well. She looked on the edge of tears, and yet I know she was very happy for Erin."

"No jealousy there?"

"Oh, some, I'm sure. No one likes to have someone else pass him up. Ernest could hardly take it. He was swearing and carrying on so, I was just glad he had that appointment so he could get out of there. Pity the poor prospect, though. I'll bet it wasn't a good meeting for Mr. Gibbons. I was unaware, by the way, that he had become top salesman in his company."

Margo stared. "I was too," she said matter-of-factly.

"Well, anyway, the boys had left me about midway through the meet, and I had to track them down by looking in all the auxiliary gyms. I found them, with the help of a janitor. They had scrounged up a volleyball or a soccer ball or something and were using it as a basketball, running with a bunch of other kids and sweating to beat the band. It was all I could do to drag them to the car, and by then Larisa had been waiting quite a while."

Margo had found the janitor on duty that night who had led Mrs. Cumiskey to the impromptu basketball game.

"Good work, Margo," Earl said in the office. "Larry, how'd you do?"

"Well, Greg and Linda embraced when it was all over, if that's what you're after."

154

We all clapped.

"And I got a few straight answers for once, though Erin was pretty stony. She didn't want to talk there but she asked me in private if she could come and talk to you, Earl. She said she'd heard good things about you from her grandmother."

"Fine. When does she want to meet?"

"After the competition tonight. Possible?"

"Sure. Where?"

"Bonnie's apartment. She's going to spend the night."

"So what kind of straight answers did you get from Greg and Linda?"

"Well, they were so impressed with the fact that each had tried to confess to protect the other that it was hard to get them to do anything but make eyes at each other."

Bonnie was listening intently, obviously pleased.

"But Greg finally admitted that he and Johnny had attended the same sales meeting Friday, and in his haste to avoid Johnny he left without picking up all his material. Johnny had brought it back to the office and when he saw Greg in the parking lot, he just called him over to the car and handed it to him. They were formal, short of cordial, according to Greg, but he did thank him, and Greg had, indeed, leaned on the car door when he picked up the stuff."

"Simple enough," Earl said.

"Yeah. Johnny's visit to Linda wasn't so simple though. It seems she had something of his that he wanted back. She gave him what for on the phone, saying that if he so much as showed up, she would make a scene he would regret. He said he was coming anyway. And he did."

"He was at Linda Gibbons's the day he died?"

"That's right."

"I'm gonna have to ask Wally how VCD missed that," Earl said.

"It was a short visit. She saw him arrive from the window and was out and down before he had even parked. She opened the passenger door and threatened him."

"She threatened him? She didn't just give back whatever the gift was?"

"No, she threatened him. She said that's why she burst into tears upon hearing of his death. To her it was as if her threat had been a prayer and she felt responsible. She still has the gift."

"What was it?"

"Just a bottle of perfume. I don't understand that. Why would a guy like Bizell want a bottle of perfume back? How much could it have cost?"

"That's the kind of man he was," Bonnie said. "That's why he was so despicable."

"What kind of perfume was it?" I asked.

"What's the difference?" Earl said.

"I just wanna know."

Margo shot me a doubletake when Larry said, "Chantilly. According to Linda, it's not even her brand. It's Erin's."

"Weird," Earl said.

"Philip," Margo said, "is that why you asked me—"

I shushed her, but Earl wouldn't let it drop. "What's

going on, Philip? Do you know something we all should know?"

"Oh, it's just a little secret that Festschrift confided in me. I don't know how important it is since so many people use that kind of perfume."

"Philip, I have never known Wally Festschrift to do anything but *trade* secrets. He never just gives them away. What'd *you* tell *him*?"

"I didn't know we had any secrets *he* didn't have," I said. Earl squinted at me, just short of contemptuously. "I think he gives secrets to people he likes and trusts. I didn't have to trade anything." Earl was cool to me for the rest of the day.

Everyone from our shop was planning to go to the meet that night. Tickets were not easy to come by. Larry was to ask Erin if she would talk to all of us, including Sergeant Festschrift. "If she knows anything more than what we've got, we have to jump on it," Earl said. "Everything's closing up on us."

I took binoculars to the Horizon that night and watched less of the gymnasts than I did the spectators. I sat with Earl and Larry while Margo and Bonnie sat with Greg and Linda Gibbons in a different section.

"I'm sorry about that secret business today, Earl," I said. "This is all it was." I took the packet out of my pocket, told him what the lab had found on Bizell's body, and pierced the plastic with my finger. "They call it Chantilly," I said.

"It makes me think of Mrs. Cumiskey," Earl said as

other spectators turned around to see where the scent was coming from.

"Yeah, I know," I said, "but don't jump to conclusions, because Larisa also uses it, and most of the girls on the team use it too because they admire her so. Erin uses it as much as anyone, and Linda has been known to borrow hers."

"I can see why you didn't think there was much to it," Earl said. "It hardly narrows our field, does it?"

"Nope."

"I still don't like the idea of your withholding something from your co-workers."

"I know, Earl, and I'm sorry. If it had turned out to be more important, I would have remembered to tell you. It won't happen again."

Chapter Thirteen

I don't believe Ernest Cumiskey knew Erin would be in uniform until the AAU team ran out from the locker room. Larisa led the way with Erin prancing right behind her, looking bright and fresh in spite of it all. I turned the glasses on the Cumiskeys, who rose with everyone else to applaud the country's best team, but when Cumiskey saw Erin his hands stopped in midair and he ranted to his wife.

She stopped clapping too and followed his pointing finger. I got the impression she attempted to soothe him.

As the girls sat next to each other in metal folding chairs on the perimeter of the floor, I focused in to see the interaction between Larisa and Erin, assuming they would be thrilled to have been reunited. But they weren't even looking at each other. And when their teammates did exceptionally well or exceptionally poorly, they might congratulate or console them, but they never exulted together, and they seemed to never even speak to each other, though they sat right next to each other.

I had seen them in meets before, talking so much and so animatedly and encouraging each other, sharing secrets, cheering the scores of everyone. This was strange. I couldn't figure it. I turned back to the Cumiskeys, who were carefully studying the competition as the lesser ranked girls performed their routines.

Mr. Cumiskey started by recording scores on his program as he did at every meet, but by the end—regardless how well or how poorly his daughter did, that program would be unrecognizable, having been used for a megaphone, a whipping post, or whatever.

When Larisa's teammates performed, he grew pensive, waiting for Larisa. When Erin was up, he was dark and moody, not ranting, not cheering, regardless. Always, until Larisa performed and he felt uncomfortable unless he stood and moved, he sat close to his wife, his arm alternately around her back, her shoulder, the back of her head.

I asked Earl to watch him while Erin performed. "He sure looks possessive, doesn't he?" Earl said. "It would seem she'd get tired of that, but he was doing the same thing when we were at their place, wasn't he?"

I nodded and took the binos back. Erin had scored under 9 on the uneven bars, and she sat quietly weeping next to Larisa, who ignored her. When Larisa was up, Erin looked the other way. The older girl scored only slightly higher than Erin, and they stood ninth and tenth at the end of the first event. Coach Adamski sat with his head in his hands. The fourth best uneven bars performer on his team had surprised him with her best score ever, but even she was only in sixth place.

To the uninitiated, it may have seemed too early to be giving up on a repeat national title, but with such a huge field and your stars off their games, it was already virtually over.

Neither Erin nor Larisa scored as high as a 9 all evening. There were four different winners of the four events. The girl from Dubuque won the all-around with a 39.15 with neither of the favorites even in the running. Ernest Cumiskey was beside himself. We discovered later that he left his keys with his wife and let her take the family home. He showed up near midnight in a cab, not entirely sober. It was a first for him.

Wally Festschrift was waiting at Bonnie's apartment when our whole gang trouped in, much more subdued than we expected. After having talked with Erin's coach earlier in the day, I was less optimistic than the others about how she might fare, but not even Adamski could have predicted that dismal showing. And what had been wrong with Larisa?

Erin was teary and sullen, quite obviously humiliated, but determined to go through with talking to Earl. They sat with Wally and Bonnie at Bonnie's dining room table with the rest of us—Larry, Margo, and me—sitting in a row on the couch. We didn't want to appear too eager to hear everything, but we were, and there was no sound but Erin's tiny voice. I couldn't get over how grownup she looked with the makeup she wore only for meets. The eyeshade and the bright lipstick didn't fit the little person and voice, but she was something to listen to.

"I wanted to talk to you, Mr. Haymeyer, because my grandma told me you might understand. I'm not as comfortable as I thought I might be with all these people here, but I guess it's all right."

"They've all been working on this case, Erin," Earl said. "Mostly because we love you and your grandmother and they'd like to see that nobody, especially you and your family, gets in trouble for something you didn't do."

"I know. And that's why I'm here. See, I know who killed Johnny. I admitted it until Sergeant Fest—"

"Festschrift."

"Uh-huh, until he tripped me up on some questions, but everybody thought I did that to protect my mother or father. I know them better than that. Neither of them could have done it. Well, maybe they could have, but they didn't, and I knew it."

"How did you know, Erin?"

"Because that thing that was used to cut Johnny's neck used to be part of my razor. But I never had it at home, so where would they get it?"

Erin looked at Bonnie and started crying. "I know why she did it. She did it because she loved me and because she didn't want to see me hurt. She didn't want to see my parents split up for good."

Earl was startled. "Honey, your grandmother has witnesses who can account for her whereabouts at the time of the murder."

"She's not accusing me," Bonnie said. "She has someone else in mind."

"Larisa," Erin said painfully. "She and I broke that razor when we were messing around. She told me to be careful when I threw it away. And I was. I threw it away at her house in the waste basket in the master bedroom where we had our slumber party."

No one spoke. Earl leaned forward and put his hand on Erin's arm, but it was Festschrift who asked the next question. "Do you remember throwing away both pieces?"

"Huh?"

"Both pieces. It broke in two, didn't it?"

"Yeah. Of course I threw away both pieces. What would anyone want with a worthless piece of plastic?"

"What, indeed," Festschrift said, standing. "Earl, there's only one more piece to this puzzle, and we can make an arrest."

"What will happen to her?" Erin asked, sobbing.

"I don't know, Erin," Earl said. "Let's just say that your friend is going to be one very sad and disappointed young woman." She was crying softly on her grandmother's shoulder when we left.

Festschrift spent most of the ride home moaning to Earl about "just two more small items, well, one not so small."

"I'll bite," Earl said.

"I wanna confirm my suspicions about the perfume, and I wanna come up with a motive."

"The motive is simple," Margo said. "Jealousy."

"But the murderer is usually jealous of the victim. If that were true in this case, Erin would be dead."

"It's more convoluted than that," Margo said.

"First tell me what *convoluted* means, and then tell me what you're talking about."

"I just mean it's more involved than simple one-on-one jealousy. The whole family is jealous of Erin's athletic superiority, whether they all admit it or not. Erin chooses the wrong place to throw away both the weapon and the

163

evidence that will be put back into her bag to implicate her. The girls have talked about murdering the man, and even put it in writing. Ironically, the night the murder is planned, Erin provides more reason than ever by destroying Larisa in every event. After that, it was as good as done. Erin would be suspected and Larisa would be left at the top of the heap.

"I like it," Festschrift said. "I mean, I don't like it, but I mean, you know what I mean."

The next morning at nine o'clock, Festschrift and Earl and I visited Mrs. Cumiskey, who was home alone. "It's very important that we talk to your husband," Wally said. "Would he be at work?"

She panicked. "Why, what is it? Has something happened to Larisa or the boys?"

"No, ma'am," he said. "I really prefer to talk to him alone first, if you don't mind."

She appeared troubled. "Well, he would be at the health club this morning and then he would arrive at work, always at ten sharp. Can't you tell me what this is about?"

"I wish I could, Mrs. Cumiskey," Festschrift said. "You won't be in the dark long, I assure you."

As she showed us to the door, Wally uncharacteristically put his hand carefully on her shoulder and up to the back of her collar, which he gently straightened. He expressed his thanks.

In the car he held out his hand to Earl and me so we could smell the heavy scent of Chantilly. "Enough to transfer to a man's skin if I touched him," he said.

We arrived at Cumiskey's office and pulled into his parking space at 9:45. It seemed a long wait, but a few seconds before ten his sleek black Oldsmobile 98 swept into the far end of the parking lot and down toward us.

From a few car lengths away, Cumiskey could see that we were in his space. He tooted twice and then laid on the horn, but when Festschrift emerged from the car, Cumiskey stopped and slowly broke into a wide grin.

"Sergeant, what're you doing here, old pal?" he said, waving and rolling down his window, as Bizell must have done the Friday night before at his rendezvous in another parking lot.

Festschrift walked briskly to the window as if to greet him warmly, the way Cumiskey always greeted everyone, but Ernest's smile froze as the sergeant's hand came out of his overcoat pocket, not with fingers extended, but as if holding something in his palm.

He reached in behind Cumiskey's neck as if to hug him, as the murderer must have done to Bizell, but Cumiskey was a wary victim and screamed, ducking as Festschrift playfully dragged a fingernail across his neck, at the same spot Bizell was mortally wounded.

"Gotcha!" the sergeant said, showing the trembling Cumiskey his empty hand.

Ernest sat up slowly and let his head rest on the steering wheel. He sobbed.

Earl and Wally joined Margo and me for dinner late that night after a full day. I could tell that Earl, at least, was

Moody Press, a ministry of the Moody Bible Institute, is designed for education, evangelization, and edification. If we may assist you in knowing more about Christ and the Christian life, please write us without obligation: Moody Press, c/o MLM, Chicago, Illinois 60610.